i

c

o

p

e

Because

by

Joseph Riippi

Portions of this text previously appeared,
sometimes in different form, in:

Electric Literature's Recommended Reading, The
Collagist, The Coffin Factory, Volume 1 Brooklyn,
and The Fiddleback.

For Lindsay

Because I wanted you to see that there is a reason for this book, that it's about something, I'm adding this preface as the last bit of my writing.

Because I wanted reading this book to be easy for you. Because I wanted to make it so you would want to find out what happens next.

Because I wanted to explain the complicated feelings I think we all have about home, or at least the places we come from, and about having children, and about God and about living and then dying, about everything we all want.

Because I wanted to make something beautiful and figure things out. Because I wanted to write fiction, but I'm not sure that I did.

Joseph Riippi, August 2013, Berlin

Part One

I want

I want my grandfather to come back to life.

I want to ask him some questions.

I want to know about the war he fought. I want to hear the stories he never told.

I want to read my grandfather the story I wrote about the time he pounded a nail into a cedar tree with his bare hand. I want to tell him how my cousins and sister and I still talk about it when we get together.

I want to know if that really happened, that bit with the nail, or if it was just one of memory's tricks.

I want to tell my children about the lake house my grandfather built with his bare hands. I want to tell them how he hammered nails with his fists and crushed huge spiders between his fingers. I want to tell them how he would do cartwheels when he was excited and couldn't contain it. I want to tell them how he would sing when he was angry and wanted not to be. I want to build a family that would make my grandfather do cartwheels for miles.

I want to sit on the lake house porch and pour a beer and clink a glass with my grandfather alive again. I want to lean back and breathe lake air and look out at the mountains and listen to my grandfather tell his version of the nail story.

I want to know what he was like before he was old. I want
to know what he did the night before his wedding. I want
to hear the war stories.

I want to know what he meant at the party for his and my
grandmother's fiftieth wedding anniversary, when he raised
a shaky hand in a salute and said, It's been a long war.

I want to know if that was a joke or if he was confused
and thought it was an actual war he was in, if he got all of
us family confused for soldiers.

I want to know what it's like to fight in a war. I want to
know what it's like to have no choice but to go and fight. I
want him to explain it to me.

I want to tell him about the last time I saw him, when he
was dying and I was eighteen and he confused me for my
father. I want to tell him what he said to me. I want to ask
if he meant what he said.

I want my own last words to count so much.

I want you to understand why I am writing this.

I want you to listen to me.

I want

I want to understand how I want so many things.

I want to be heard. I want to be remembered. I want to be happy as my grandfather was.

I want to be remembered as happy and loving.

I want to be remembered as gracious and kind and a wonderful writer.

I want to have presence, like a great actor on a bare stage. I want to have prescience. I want to have stature. I want gravitas. I want grace.

I want to learn how to cartwheel.

I want to learn how to sing.

I want to live heroically.

I want to know how many people my grandfather watched die in the war. I want to ask him how many last words he remembered.

I want my family to be proud of me. I want my wife to be proud of me.

I want to have a party on our fiftieth anniversary, and I want to say something like, It's been too short.

I want to think of something better than that to say.

I want my wife to live a happy and joyful life.

I want our children and their children to be happy, to live lives remembered joyfully in songs and in stories with great love and loud laughter and pride in their surnames.

I want, really, the same that you want.

I want, badly, for you to love me.

I want

I want, on our fiftieth anniversary, for my wife and me to spend the day telling family stories of our adventures. I want my grandchildren to know everything about me.

I want to pound a nail into a cedar tree with my bare hand.

I want you to understand what I'm trying to say here.

I want to know if you're hearing me.

I want this explained back to me because I don't know, not exactly, what I'm trying to say.

I want to look back on my life and remember it happily and lovingly and proudly, and if I have to remember my life differently, if that will make me happier, then yes, I want to remember differently.

I want to remember doing cartwheels through Italian mountains alongside my grandfather in a war. I want to remember singing away our anger at enemies during fire-fights. I want to remember singing at God in the aftermath. I want to remember cowering and trying to sleep in wet trenches.

I want

I want to relive crawling under a blanket as a child. I want
to relive the smell of the fabric and carpet.

I want to feel safe.

I want to relive getting tucked tight into bed at night. I want
to relive picture books and board books being read to me. I
want to relive skinning my knee on the driveway
and my mother's fast running.

I want to relive Christmas mornings and birthdays. I want
to relive bicycles and summer vacations. I want to remember having always done the right thing.

I want to remember harder, and by harder I mean I want
to remember better, more sharply, with more specificity
and clarity and sense. I want razor-edge thinking like
for cutting up filmstrips.

I want to remember smells and tastes simultaneously,
sounds and sights simultaneously, faces and names, feelings
and emotions, a great grand mess of sense. I want remembering to be like reliving. I want to relive what
I've lived through already.

I want to relive my wedding as a guest. I want to relive
my first bike crash as my father. I want to relive my first
taste of ice cream as the woman who scooped it. I want to
relive my first smell of wet grass clippings. I want to relive
my first smell of dirt, of gouda, of cookies baking. I want

to relive every embarrassment and triumph. I want to edit the past like the draft of a novel written from memory.

I want to remember away the wrong bits. I want to also re-member away the bits that don't fit, the bits I don't like, the split infinitives and illogical turns of plot or undeveloped character. I want choices as to how I remember, but I don't want to be conscious of choosing.

I want to read this fifty years from now and not change a word.

I want finality. I want excellence. I want perfection.

I want to know if you are understanding this.

I want to know if you also want these things.

I want to be more specific. I want to be happy, but I don't want to know that I've reached happiness. I want to be surprised by my happiness. I want to be sad sometimes so as to have a comparative kind of happiness. I want a hap-piness that is so full and so real and sustained it becomes stasis, just how I am. I want to make my wife happy in a way that's higher and hardier than my own happiness. I want a happiness that grows between us, between my wife and me, like a tree in endless blossom.

I want us to radiate happiness and ride on it like waves.

I want my wife to understand me better than I understand myself. I want to be a better husband.
I want to be the best husband.

I want to feel as though I've led a full life. I want people to cry at my funeral. I want the children to smile.

I want to die painlessly without regret. I want my grandchildren and great-grandchildren to be proud they've descended from me. I want them to tell stories of how I cartwheeled and sang, of how much I loved and was loved.

I want to feel less narcissistic for writing this.

I want to be honest in writing this, even if honesty means narcissistic feelings.

I want to be a better son. I want to make my parents proud.

I want

I want to feel depressed less.

I want to not care about money. I want to not want to be
rich. I want to be proud without arrogance. I want to be
rich without money. I want to not want a nice car. I want
to not want a nicer apartment. I want to be content with
what I have. I want to be being honest right now. I want an
extra of everything, just in case. I want to be more aware
of everything good I already have. I want to say,
Enough, and mean it.

I want to sigh satisfactorily at the end of each day. I want
to finish each day feeling like a farmer who has seeded a
field. I want to watch something grow and blossom so I
can say, I did that, this was my doing,
and I might feel proud.

I want accomplishment and pride.
I want ease and comfort.

I want a job I can do in my apartment, and I want an
apartment in the city and a house on an island. I want a
getaway place somewhere in Northern Italy with olive trees
and fields of herbs, leaves blowing fragrant in river breeze.

I want to learn how to make wine. I want to learn how to
make shoes. I want to tell people I am a cobbler. I want to
be a chef. I want to paint. I want to sculpt. I want to make
sandals. I want to make rocking horses. I want to design
decks of cards and umbrellas. I want to carve wooden

blocks of the alphabet and teach my children to spell out
their names. I want to carve a magnolia leaf from marble.
I want to make beautiful things. I want the world to be
better because I lived in it. I want the world to be more
beautiful because I lived in it.

I want to be thinner. I want to be more attractive. I want to
be healthier for myself and for my wife. I want to be a better lover. I want to be a long-distance runner. I want to be
a better brother. I want to be a better friend. I want certain
people out of my life forever. I want to run away.

I want to not feel guilty about not living close to my family.
I want to not feel guilty about having said I want certain
people out of my life forever.

I want to know if you know who you are.

I want my family to understand that my choosing to live
far away is not because I don't love them. I want to always
tell people the truth. I want to always write the truth. I
want it to be easier for me to always tell people the truth.
I want people to like me. I want to always be the best at
whatever I do. I want to not always be so competitive. I
want supremacy. I want to not always want so much. I
want to not feel like writing this is something I have to do
to stay sane. I want to stay sane just by breathing. I want
to stay sane without thinking, I want to stay sane without
pills. I want to not feel so much like shit if I don't write. I
want to not feel so much like shit in general.

I want to not feel so much like shit when I do write or
because of what I've written.
I want to not write the word shit anymore.

I want to not remember that I tried to kill myself.

I want to relive and remember that day and night I tried
to kill myself differently. I want to change the before and
after. I want to not still sometimes want to die. I want to
not think about that, but I want to remember it actually
sometimes still so that it makes me appreciate being alive
and capable of remembering.

I want to know if anyone else in my family
ever tried to die.

I want to know if my grandfather ever held his own rifle
to his head during the war and thought how about how the
bullet might feel, if he'd hear it, if he'd smell it.

I want to know if his cartwheels were ever just a way of
shedding tears so as not to show his weakness.

I want to just fucking say what I am trying to say. I want
to not wonder about this anymore. I want to not know if I
actually meant to die. I want to move on.

I want

I want you to understand how good it feels to pass a blooming magnolia on your way to work while holding your wife's hand.

I want you to know the love of your life. I want you to marry. I want you to believe the world is a beautiful place.

I want you to feel what it's like to pass a blooming magnolia and have your body fill up with some kind of joy, inflatingly, warm and tender like under a blanket in childhood. I want you to know true love, and I want to know what you love. I want to know what it's like to be the one who truly loves you. I want to know what it's like to be the person who knows all your secrets.

I want to know all your secrets, and I want you to know mine.

I want to know the secrets of the old woman who lives in the single-family brownstone on 22nd Street with that blooming magnolia before its stoop. I want to know what she's cooking on those nights we see her through the front window, framed between exposed brick and steel pot racks and basil plants. I want to know how she affords that massive home. I want to know her grey-haired husband's name. I want to know her name. I want to know if I will recognize their names. I want to know if they are famous actors I just don't recognize outside a screen. I want to know if they are famous writers. I want them to be writers. I want them to be people just like me who worked hard

and were lucky and kept at it. I want a correspondence
with them. I want to exchange postcards. I want to type-
write carbon-copy letters and read them only once they've
been forgotten. I want to know if they raised children in
that brownstone. I want to have been a child in a five-story
brownstone, playing hide-and-seek, skinning knees
on so many stairs.

I want to solve mysteries in a brownstone from a children's
book. I want to know what it's like to have a child. I want
to reread all the children's books. I want to know what it's
like to watch a daughter laugh. I want to know what it's
like to watch a son throw a baseball in a summer field.

I want to teach someone the elementary things, like
paper-airplane building and pencil cursive, long division
and duck-and-cover. I want to teach algebra, the different
sides of an equation. I want to teach fractions and fractals.
I want to teach verb conjugation and subject, predicate,
direct object. I want to scan sentences with a red pencil.
I want to write sharp paragraphs on a chalkboard. I want
to oversee a recess. I want to catch someone falling from
a jungle gym. I want to play in the tractor tires. I want to
play foursquare and wall ball. I want to play jacks. I want
to play quarters. I want to play tackle football in a muddy
empty lot. I want to play basketball on a netless hoop with
a plywood backboard. I want to climb chain link fences
and break into high school gymnasiums. I want to play
two-hand touch in the street. I want grass stains on my
knees and elbows. I want grass stains on my jeans and
cashmere. I want grass stains on my cheeks and a chipped
tooth. I want whiter teeth. I want self-cleaning clothes. I
want bedding that smells of dryer sheets. I want a plaid
picnic blanket and wine-filled basket. I want to chase

grasshoppers and praying mantises up a hill like a poem.

I want to know if mantises are preying or praying. I want to know the verb-root separation between to prey and to pray. I want to prey like a mantis and pray like a grasshopper.

I want to grow very small and ride on a helicopter seed falling from a cedar.

I want to tell you about the time a childhood friend and I climbed high into a cedar tree with pellet guns slung over our shoulders. I want to tell you how we rested in steady branches, how we whispered, Lock and load, like imagined soldiers, how my friend whispered, Fire, and shot that mean old bastard farmer who lived next door in the eye. I want to tell you this didn't happen, that I don't remember the police being called, the crying, the I-didn't-mean-to's. I want to tell you it had been my friend's idea, that it had been my friend's cat that the mean old bastard killed with a rattrap. I want forgiveness for this, too. I want to say confession. I want to hear confession.

I want to tell you how the counseling center in college gave me pills that were supposed to make me feel better and how instead they just made me feel nothing at all, which was actually worse than the feeling that made me walk into the center in the first place. I want to tell you how someone called the center to say they were worried about me, concerned for my life, and how the counselor only told me about that after everything had happened. I want to know who called. I want to know what they saw me do or heard me say, or didn't, that made them call.

I want to know if I still sometimes do, or don't do, those things.

I want to not ever have tried alcohol. I want to not ever have smoked a cigarette. I want to not ever drink alcohol or smoke a cigarette again. I want to smoke pot, just once, just to see what it's like. I want to not be afraid that I'll like it too much. I want a less addictive personality, but I still want routine. I want to not write about this any more. I want to not repeat myself.

I want to confess on a highway billboard that I tried to kill myself and failed. I want to confess with light projection on the sides of tall buildings that I ate a bottle of pills but a best friend saved my life. I want massive forgiveness. I want total pardon.

I want to cry so badly right now.

I want to learn how to sing these awfulest things away.

I want

I want to confess I've never given it all I've got, never left it all on the field, never given a hundred and ten percent. I want to give my wife and our children my all. I want to die having left it all on the field.

I want to do everything I can. I want to do my best. I want to do everything, everything, everything, everything—and then I want to do it again and again and again and again.

I want to live and keep living. I want to do more.

I want

I want to tell you all the things I want to have done.

I want to collect leaves in autumn on a brick college campus and press them between the pages of a paperback guide on arachnids. I want to spend a weekend trapped alone in a library.

I want to dangle from the minute hand of a clock tower at a quarter past the hour and listen through the ticking for approaching sirens.

I want to drive an ambulance at full speed down an avenue. I want to take it up on two wheels, screeching around a corner and running the red.

I want to carry a stretcher up flights and flights of burning stairs in a fire. I want to do chest compressions on the old woman in a brownstone while shouting Don't you die on me, Don't you die on me, Don't you die on me.

I want to cut someone loose from the belt they used to hang themselves. I want to catch them in my arms and say, It's okay, it's okay, as they gasp. I want to stick my fingers down the throat of a best friend who swallowed a bottle of pills. I want to hug someone tightly and have them hug me back.

I want to sit with my grandfather during the coldest nights of his war and comfort him with true stories about his future.

I want to deliver a baby in a taxicab.

I want to save lives and make new ones.

I want to change the tire of a stranger's station wagon on the turnpike shoulder in a rainstorm.

I want to run across a four-lane highway and lie down on the yellow line and listen to the tires moving past. I want to know what it's like to be hit by a car.

I want to know what it's like to be driving the car that hits someone. I want to know what it's like to cause a truly tragic, deadly accident. I want to know what it's like to accidentally take life and keep on living.

I want to shoot target practice at camouflaged mannequins in a wheat field while magnolias sway pink and purple in the distance and a platoon of soldiers cartwheels past with melodic battle cries in their mouths.

I want to know what it's like to hold a new baby in a hospital delivery room. I want to know what it's like to hold a four-day-old baby in the middle of the night near a crib and realize the reality of fatherhood. I want to know what it's like to be a newborn baby. I want assurances that I can and will be a good father.

I want to know the cause of crib death. I want to know how conscious a newborn baby is, if they are as conscious as adults can be, only without memory.

I want to go back to school to be a neuroscientist. I want

to uncover the secrets of memory making. I want to peer
into microscopes at neurons and axons and the sparks they
make between. I want to watch the oldest memories like
dusty home movies projected on a sheet hung
up in an attic.

I want to see my first steps, my first words, my first kiss
with my wife, my first time driving a stick shift, every one
of my first days of school, my first dance, my first time
holding hands, my first Christmas wake-up, my first morning with a new puppy, my first time wetting the bed, my
last time wetting the bed, my first time using a toilet like
a big boy, my first computer, my first smile, my first joke,
my first sentence, my first book read to me at bedtime, my
first book read on my own, my first swim, my first jump-
ing jack, my first somersault, my first time standing up on
water-skis, my first time pulling a trout from the lake at my
grandparents' house, my first time helping my grandfather
build something, my first time helping put up the Christmas lights, my first time playing in a sprinkler, my first time
playing catch, my first game of cards, my first basketball
shot, my first swing of a baseball bat, my first time eating
snow, my first play of my first football game under the
bright lights of the stadium, my first failure, my first embarrassment, my first lesson, my first pride.

I want to capture each of my memories and wants in a jam
jar like a child catches fireflies, and I want to keep them in
glowing cabinets, ready to open whenever
I feel like reliving.

I want

I want to tell you about where I was born, Seattle, the Pacific Northwest, and how because I was born there and grew up there and left there, the music and movies and art from there belong to me more than to you.

I want to tell you about the famous things I remember that you already recognize, the flannel and rain and romantic comedies. I want to tell you the names of the yellow-slickered men throwing salmon for photographers, the histories of the neon signs and the tragedies of failed coffee shops no one outside Capitol Hill remembers. I want to tell you about the puddles in the cobblestones and how they reflect the white sky and plaid and no umbrellas, ever.

I want you to remember your favorites of all those songs written by the wet-hooded musicians who splashed and laughed beneath my white sky. I want to have helped load-in amplifiers and drum kits in exchange for beer and tickets to the concerts I was too young to see.

I want mosh pits and tinnitus. I want crowd surfing and a boot to the face.

I want you to hear this, and hear me, and know exactly what I'm talking about. I want you to know without me having to tell you what song I'm thinking about right now.

I want to play guitar on the roof of the Pike Place Market. I want to play guitar while sitting in an evergreen. I want to fly high up through white clouds like swimming

in the Sound. I want to float back down like a cedar seed
dropped upon the Sound's surface and then, water-logged,
slowly sink to the bottom with all the other needles and
leaves in the mud. I want to rest and breathe and find out
if there, at the darkest part of the Sound, deeper than
any family grave, is where I belong. I want to wave at the
octopi. I want to wave at the orcas. I want to sing out and
watch the bubbles rise like leaves falling up.

I want to show you my school-portrait fashions and how-
to-play-guitar songbooks, the commemorative mugs clog-
ging the cupboards. I want you to learn to play the famous
power chord riffs with me. I want you to head bang. I want
you to feel the rush of blood.

I want to watch a movie with you and point out the restaurant in the background where I had my twelfth birthday
party. I want to take you to the first famous coffee shop. I
want to drink coffee with you and tell you about my grandfather and how he came to this country on a boat before
the war. I want to show you the postcard he sent from
New York City when he first arrived, the one that's a painting of a blooming magnolia with a brownstone beside it
and the Statue of Liberty in its backyard.

I want to stand with you atop the Space Needle, as my
grandfather did with me on my fifth birthday, the first one
I can remember. I want him to put his arms around us. I
want him to point out for us the biggest mountain. I want
him to tell us his early stories, about when he was a ski
trooper from Finland and new husband
to my grandmother.

I want to have known my grandmother then, when she

smiled and put a hand to her heart and hung a flag with a
blue army star in the kitchen window. I want to have coffee
with her and listen to her and hear her tell me about her
new soldier husband. I want to hear the versions she might
tell of all my grandfather's made-up stories. I want to tell
her the versions I remember and check them
against her memory for facts.

I want to make my grandmother laugh when I tell of how
her husband told us grandkids he worked for Santa when
he was in the army, how most men spent the war fighting,
but he was charged with finding the Clauses a summer
home to vacation in, a getaway that was still snowy like the
North Pole, but warm enough to be a break from it.

I want to drive my children through the Puyallup Valley
when they're very young, and I want to point up to the
mountain and tell the kids how their Great-Grandfather
Riippi built a summer cabin there for Santa, in the white
patch between the green and the blue, with a great magnolia tree in the yard that was always pink and purple in blossom, so the Clauses and elves could always find their way
home through the snow. I want to tell them that someday
we'll climb the mountain together and find it.

I want to describe for you what really happened on the
mountain, how that's where the Tenth Mountain Division
trained in the early years of the war. I want to show you
their teams of pack-mules like reindeer, their armory of
small and large guns like a toyshop. I want to show you
their tents, perched just above the tree line, where the
rocks were white as the snow, and the snow was hard as
rocks, and there was no pink or purple beauty in sight.

I want to read to you the Bible verses and curse words the men scratched into their skis like football players. I want to watch the games of hot potato they played with live grenades along the glacier cliffs. I want to know what it was like to sit around a fire and wonder if I'd ever have to kill or what it feels like to be blown up. I want to know what it was like to be my grandfather's friend.

I want to stand atop the mountain with him and look back at you watching from the Needle on the Sound, from outer space or a pink-purple morning sky.

I want to sing out ho-ho-ho to my wife and children looking up from the valley. I want to holler and smile and wave at them to join.

I want to be better at explaining my complicated feelings about home, or what was home, this place I come from.

I want to know why I keep wanting to cry while I write this.

I want

I want to tell you more about the Puyallup Valley, thirty
miles south along Puget Sound, the town my parents
moved to before I was old enough to remember. I want to
tell you about the view from the house we lived in on the
hill and the berry-farm rows laid out beneath it. I want to
tell you how the farms looked like the weave of my grandmother's placemats leading up to the
great white mountain.

I want to remember the first time I saw that mountain so
that I can tell you about it now. I want you to understand
how beautiful it looked from the front windows of that
first house, the one we moved from later, in high school.
I want to tell you how when I see that same mountain in
movies or paintings, I feel just a little bit like that movie-
maker or painter stole something from me.

I want to know what the view from that window
looks like now.

I want to know why I feel so possessive over it.
I want to understand this feeling better. I want to know
if you get this feeling, too. I want to know how you feel
about the place you call home.

I want to explain to you how the name Riippi was a powerful name in high school sports across South Puget Sound.
I want you to understand how proud I was to be called
Riippi when I sat in my first-day freshman classes. I want
to show you newspaper clippings of all of us Riippi kids

lined up in our leather letter jackets like a row of armor
suits or doppelgangers in a police line-up.

I want to go down the row telling you which ones went to
jail and which ones I remember best and which ones have
kids and which one—me, the only one—hasn't
come home yet.

I want to go back more often than I do, more often than
holidays and life events. I want to visit for reasons greater
than some metaphorical sense of needing to water the
roots that remain, this kind of obligatory maintenance
that isn't love or interest so much as avoidance of shame. I
want love for reasons beyond bloodline or responsibility.

I want to confess the sadness that last sentence carries.

I want more than confession now. I want this book to be
more than a list of wantings. I want it to be a love letter,
a prayer, a purge.

I want it to be a song that carries away all of my
shames and sadness.

I want

I want to tell you about the song I heard today in the Los Angeles airport, and how upon hearing it I could smell the leather couch in the basement of that Puyallup house, the one on the hill above the berry fields. I want to know what happened to all those tape cassettes we kept in boxes beneath the stereo in the living room. I want to sing along to the favorite-song family mixtapes we made for road trips.

I want to tell you about the red flannel shirt my wife bought me at a sporting goods store in Texas, when we were visiting her parents and her father and I went off in search of birdseed. I want to tell you about the great swell of pride in my gut when her mother said, Now that's a perfect Seattle shirt for Joe!

I want to tell you how many rainy days in New York City someone has said to me, You must love this weather, with a bit of disdain. I want to tell you it happens every time it rains, but you would think I'm being hyperbolic.

I want to tell you about the jillion-gazillion umbrellas I've broken on New York City streets, and how I can't remember ever owning an umbrella in Puyallup because I always had a hood on my sweatshirt or jacket.

I want to know where hometown pride comes from.

I want to know more about how memory works. I want to know more about how rain works. I want to tell you about the time I fell off my bike in Puyallup and cartwheeled over the handlebars into a puddle. I want to know more about farming and geology. I want to know how my grandfather got all those pack-mules onto the side of a mountain. I want to know where the army got all those pack-mules in the first place. I want to know if he named the mules. I want to know if he sang to them. I want to know if he loved them.

I want to know what the view is really like from the top of Mt. Rainier.

I want to know the exact date and time that Mt. Rainier will erupt, because it's going to happen, for sure. I want to know if they still have those volcano evacuation emergency drills in the Puyallup schools. I want to know if my family will be long gone by the time it actually blows.

I want to know what it'll look like, when the top of the mountain goes up in muddy flames.

I want to know what's happening inside that mountain-volcano right now.

I want to never stop learning or wanting to learn.

I want to go back to school and be a genius.

I want

I want to have paid better attention in science classes.

I want to know what makes magnolias pink-purple and white instead of orange, instead of gray.

I want to have, maybe, applied to medical school.

I want to know what it's like to be a doctor. I want to know what it's like to be a lifeguard. I want to save someone from drowning or untie someone from train tracks in the old west or just save anyone from anything before they slowly bleed out. I want to make tourniquets out of bath towels and perform tracheotomies with ballpoint pens.

I want more interesting stories to tell. I want to know what it's like to spend my days saving lives. I want to know what it's like to end a day covered in the blood of people whose lives I've saved, or failed to. I want bloodstains on my white jacket and fingers. I want to shake hands with the father of a child whose life I've saved. I want to take off bloody gloves backwards like surgeons do. I want to know what it's like to be a fireman. I want to know what it's like to be a firefighter running up the stairs of a burning building.

I want to be a dalmatian hanging my head out the side of a fire truck with a siren blazing.

I want to be a lab with its tongue hanging out after a summer run. I want to catch a Frisbee between my teeth.

I want to catch a tennis ball in my mouth. I want to piss on a fire hydrant while someone says, Good boy. I want to know what it's like to be a dog that is loved. I want to sleep in front of fireplaces or at the foot of a bed. I want someone to knit me a sweater. I want to know what it's like to be a cat, but just for a day. I want to work in an independent bookstore. I want to be the strange cat that lurks among the stacks of the largest independent bookstores. I want to be a cat that reads but never speaks.

I want to work in a music shop. I want to rent out band and orchestra instruments to aspiring school children.

I want to hold the hands of a dying luthier. I want blacksmiths to teach me their art. I want carpenters to teach me their art. I want to make more with my hands.

I want to build watches and laser pointers. I want a pair of gloves that doesn't make my hands sweat.

I want to build a grandfather clock with my bare hands. I want to chop the trees for the wood and fire the sand for the face. I want to polish wood with bare hands and rags of my grandfather's old shirts.

I want to forge the clock's weights and pendulum from Finnish pewter or steel. I want to fill the belly of the clock with the letters and books I'll write in my lifetime.

I want a lock for the clock face assembled from my grandmother's trinkets. I want pieces of Finland in my grandfather clock.

I want to slice my finger to bleed into the polish. I want

pieces of my heart and family in my grandfather clock. I want to spend my whole life building this clock. I want its ticking to start the moment my heart's ticking stops.

I want the last thing I see in this world to be the first tick of the clock I spent my lifetime making. I want the clock's lock to be a mystery. I want some descendant of mine to forge her own key. I want the belly of the clock to be a great and beautiful discovery.

I want my family to visit the clock after I've died. I want the clock to be my tombstone. I want my family to visit the mines where the Finnish pewter or steel was dug up for the weights, to want to know where and how this clock was built, to want to know how I lived and what I did while I was alive.

I want someone to tell them I loved my wife and children above all.

I want the ticking of the clock to keep time with our singing.

I want

I want to visit the mine that yield the white gold for my wedding band.

I want to bite into a gold coin to test its truth. I want my front two teeth to be real, not porcelain. I want to be capable of performing my own dentistry. I want to call someone toothless in an argument without laughing.

I want the experience and wisdom of an aged, rugged cowboy. I want to cross Texas and the Great Plains on horseback. I want to fire a six-shooter down Main Street at high noon in a duel. I want to feel what it's like to be scalped. I want to drink whiskey in an old saloon. I want to play cards with a gunslinger. I want to join a posse. I want to drive cattle to water across a panhandle. I want to know what it's like to have tuberculosis. I want to play piano in a Wild West barroom. I want to be a travelling actor. I want to ride in a caravan of wagons, barrels of guns sticking out from under tarps. I want to roll down a hill in a barrel. I want to float down a river in a barrel. I want to barrel off Niagara and splash majestically. I want to catch someone by the collar as they jump off a bridge. I want to pull them back, buy them coffee, tell them a sad life is more interesting than a peaceful death.

I want a great wit.

I want someone regal and commanding to teach me the art of conversation and presence. I want to perform grand monologues on stage. I want to keep your attention. I

want you rapt with interest and eagerness and yearning.
I want to have lunch with the President and talk about
language, not politics.

I want to know what it's like to be any race other than
white. I want to know what it's like to be anyone other
than me. I want to know what it's like to be a woman or
transgendered. I want to know what it's like to be very
poor. I want to know what it's like to be extremely rich. I
want to know how different my life would be had I grown
up just one house down from the house that I did. I want
to know how different my life would be had I been born
exactly one year earlier. I want to know if I would have
still met my wife had I been a sophomore and she been
a senior. I want to know if I would have died in a plane
crash, or if there has been some other fatal catastrophe
I have otherwise avoided and just never known about. I
want to know all the possibilities that could have been,
even if these are endless. I want endless knowing. I want to
know the finiteness of the universe. I want to know if the
attraction between objects of mass is more than gravity. I
want to know if gravity is actually soul.

I want to know if gravity is actually love, unconquerable
and constant and mysterious, or if this is just coincidence
and me stretching meaning. I want to keep
stretching meaning.

I want a cup of coffee, right now.

I want

I want to visit coffee fields in South America.

I want to hike the hills on the shady sides and taste the raw
cherry. I want to visit the coffee fields in Malaysia and the
parts of Sumatra where the famous cats, a college friend
once told me about, roam and scatter.

I want to visit that friend more or at least one more time.

I want to tell you about those fun days our freshman year,
when that friend and I played guitar for a youth group
at a church near campus. I want to tell you how we led
sing-alongs to worship songs in open-E tuning. I want to
tell you about the brightness of our brand new guitar
strings, how we bought them with pittance paychecks from
the local coffee shop. I want to tell you how we listened
to professional worship songs over the sound system. I
want to tell you about the atheist owner, who tolerated the
church music so long as we didn't proselytize, Just love
each other, he said, You don't need a god to know love's
the way to live, he said. I want to tell you how we were
good at that, at being happy and loving, and how that was
all those songs were about, really, just love, and they were
simple and beautiful. I want to tell you how I love those
songs still. I want to play them again sometimes,
and I do, just sitting around tinkering on that same
guitar I had then but with grittier strings.

I want to do more with the guitar than sit lazy in
front of the television's late-night news and serialized

sit-coms, not sleeping but remembering a time I played
and sang to a crowd of five hundred screaming teens.

I want to know if you know the feeling of fingers stiffen-
ing along old strings, slimy with dead skin and
something like rust.

I want to know if that rust-colored stuff is what makes
my guitar strings now sound deader now than they did
back then, or if it's something more emotional. I want to
know if it was God who made music then so bright and
full, sparkly with love and hope and joy, whatever it is that
makes born-agains glow as if pregnant with faith.

I want to tell you how I bent and howled over that guitar,
singing praise songs to God or just that feeling of goodness I believed was Him. I want to tell you how much I
really did believe, and thought of myself as some kind of
soldier when singing, a soldier like my grandfather screaming rosaries deep in a trench as bombs fell all around.

I want just to remember the fun of it, too, the reason
it's called playing.

I want to sing again. I want to play for a crowd that ani-
mated again. I want to know if I really believed in god or
if I just liked believing in something. I want to know if I
really loved those people I prayed with or if I just liked
that we were kind to one another. I want to know what
happened to those people. I want to know if they hated
me after I left. I want to know if they think I am going to
hell for having left. I want to know if I am going to hell.

I want to know if anyone actually deserves hell.

I want

I want to relive that camping trip the church group took, when I made out with one of the other counselors in the magnolia-less woods and she told me she liked the Jesus she saw in me. I want to know what she saw. I want to know if she actually meant Jesus Christ was in me or if it was just her way of saying I was a nice guy. I want to know what she is doing now. I want her to be doing well. I want her to find Jesus in somebody, the way she wanted or at least seemed to want. I want my children to believe in something greater than themselves.

I want to go to a Christian rock festival. I want to go camping more often. I want to see a god in the wilderness sky. I want to climb an Appalachian mountain. I want to climb a rocky, snowcapped peak. I want to stand on a glacier and look out on the valley it carved.

I want to tell you how that first friend I played guitar with is gay now, how he told me over a cup of coffee last year, and how I wanted to ask him if he still believes in god, and if so, if it's the same god he believed in back when we used to sing together.

I want to know if the god I believe in now is the same God I believed in back then. I want to know if there are different gods to believe in now than there were back then or if today it's the same God, and it's just a matter of he and I learning to understand that God better, or worse, with time.

I want to have asked my friend this, but I was too uncomfortable and afraid of all the years that had passed since we'd last seen each other.

I want to know if we all believe in the same god, even if that god is an absence or fiction, capital or lowercase.

I want to know what my friend would have said to that.

I want to know what he'll say after reading this.

I want

I want to be everything.

I want to be a farmer. I want to be a teacher. I want to be a surgeon. I want to be a mechanic. I want to spend a summer weekend working on a car in a driveway. I want to listen to a baseball game while drinking beers. I want to open the hood of a steaming car and know what's going on. I want to be handy. I want to fix plumbing. I want to be self-sufficient. I want to be self-motivated. I want to be a football coach. I want to invent new ways of training with tractor tires. I want my football team to tow a train engine along a track for a mile. I want to yell at them to dig in. I want to yell at them through an orange traffic cone. I want to inspire the minds of the youth. I want to change someone's life for the better. I want a life coach. I want a personal trainer. I want a gym in my apartment building. I want a doorman. I want laundry in my apartment. I want a bigger pot for my ficus. I want original moldings and perfectly level floorboards. I want a waffle iron like those in the college dining hall. I want to do college over again as a history major or religion major. I want to be a pilot. I want to be an astronaut. I want to go to Space Camp. I want to be a film director. I want to be an actor. I want to be a photographer, cinematographer, documentarian, video artist. I want to be on Broadway. I want to be a dancer. I want to be a ballerino. I want to take up the violin again. I want to take up the piano again. I want to take up model rocket building. I want to not have given up the violin for basketball when I was in the seventh grade. I want to play professional sports. I want to care about professional sports so that I have something to talk about with the men at parties or in the office who just assume that I know these things. I want to fish more. I want to learn to be a better fisherman. I want to learn every language. I want a fish tank of lake trout. I want a fish tank of catfish. I want a fish tank of algae and crawdads and perch, two of each, a male and female, like a tiny ark. I want to learn to bake bread. I want to break bread with a million others. I want to be a stay-at-home dad. I want to be a great father. I want a bigger apartment before I become a father. I want my child or children to love me and respect me.

I want my son, when he is in the sixth grade and asked to write, as I was, an end-of-the-year list of favorite things, I want him to write My Dad, as I did. I want my daughter to write My Mom on her list of favorite things. I want them to have difficulty deciding between my wife and me.

I want our children to never go hungry. I want our children to research both our families to find a shared lineage. I want our ancestries to cross at some ancient time. I want our ancestors to have been of some same village in Scandinavia half a thousand years ago, our so-many-great grandparents to have been great childhood friends. I want to go back in time and watch them digging up farm soil together and laughing. I want to watch them carrying well water in wooden buckets and singing folks songs at each other. I want to see them separated by war or climate, only to be brought back together again this many centuries later, in the sprinkler-splashing and backseat-singing of our children.

I want to tell you more about my grandparents who lived

in the lake house, with the cedar trees marked with nails in the yard. I want to tell you how their faucets and showers spit water only from the lake for so many years, water you shouldn't drink, they said, but was fine for showering or washing your hands before eating. I want to tell you how when they visited us in our house upon the hill they would bring big plastic jugs to fill with water from our garden hose. I want to tell you how this was the same hose I was told not to drink from, not because it wasn't drinkable but because my mother didn't like it when we drank without a glass. I want to tell you how, when I asked my father why grandfather filled those jugs with hose water every time he visited, he said it was because my grandfather was secretly in charge of making sure the lake didn't run out of water, and it hadn't rained enough lately.

I want to tell you how I used to imagine my grandparents out at the end of the dock when they got home after their visits, pouring water from our house into the lake in the middle of the night. I want to tell you how my grandfather would tip the jugs one after the other while my grand-mother stood guard to make sure no one saw. I want to tell you how in the summertime when we went swimming with the neighbor kids, I felt like our family owned more of the lake than they did, because we had filled it ourselves, because the lake was something our family had built and maintained, how it was something our family loved most, how it was our shared secret.

I want family to be my favorite thing.

I want

I want my wife and me to visit Ireland and trace her ancestral roots. I want us to visit Norway and breathe in the northern sky our deepest ancestors shared. I want us to take cooking classes from the old women in villages stirring great pots over open flames. I want to take a ferry to Finland, learn the taste of reindeer.

I want us to teach our children where they come from. I want to help my children with their homework, but only if they ask. I want my children not to need help with their homework.

I want my children to ride orange bicycles down tree-lined streets. I want to watch them make bike jumps from sheets of plywood and cinder blocks. I want to watch them pretend to fly.

I want to sit with our children and build castles from blocks. I want to watch their imaginations take shape. I want to teach our children to read. I want to read them our favorite books as they fall asleep. I want them to struggle to stay awake, yearning for one more chapter, one more page, always.

I want to know what their night-lights will look like. I want to explain to them how glow-in-the-dark works.

I want to write a children's book. I want to write a picture book. I want to be an illustrator. I want to color with crayons. I want to make a construction paper picture of my future family and duct tape it to the refrigerator. I want my job to give letter grades on assignments. I want straight-A's.

I want to take the SATs now that there's a different point scale. I want to go to art school. I want to learn the chemistry behind painting with oils, the chemistry behind cooking great stocks and stews. I want to make Thanksgiving dinner for my family, the stuffing from scratch and the pie crusts by hand. I want to go on a turkey shoot. I want to design flatware and place cards. I want to paint wineglasses and candlesticks. I want to dip candles in a basement and hang them from a clothesline to dry. I want to make crab dip. I want to make spinach dip.

I want to hold the heart of an artichoke in my hand and feel its beating. I want to hold the heart of an artichoke next to a child's ear and ask them if they can hear the love in it. I want to grill asparagus with fresh olive oil in a snowstorm. I want to recreate a family vacation with my wife and our parents and sisters. I want to do all the same things we did back as kids.

I want to tell you about a condo timeshare in Eastern Washington, the unit number F5 where my father taught me to barbecue with charcoal. I want to go back there with my own children and in-laws, and I want my father to reteach us all to fish. I want my mother to retake us shopping for sandals in town. I want to refall asleep early from eating too much pizza. I want to regut a trout with a steak knife and garden hose. I want to rewake very early to parasail, and I want to rechicken out. I want daytime minigolf with my cousins and flashlight tag after dark. I want to rerent VHS tapes and restay up past my bedtime. I want to recount out-of-state license plates on the car ride through the mountains, and I want to re-eat drive thru fast food halfway home. I want to reride a bus back to school in September wearing a souvenir t-shirt.

I want to watch my children doing all of these things for the very first time.

I want to anticipate trips to that timeshare like I did back then. I want to relive the feeling of freedom I had back then. I want to relive the feeling of potential and surety. I want to relive the evenings with no homework. I want to relive going outside to play. I want to relive those years when the empty half-acre lot down the street was full of mystery and danger, when it seemed so large and foreboding that all of us neighborhood kids called it The Woods.

I want

I want to spend an hour each day making arts and crafts. I want to spend an hour each day writing one-page book reports in number 2 pencil on wide-ruled paper. I want to groan at writing cursive and the extra few lines of college-ruled requirements. I want to feel smarter for using college-ruled paper. I want to feel mature and privileged for writing in pen. I want to doodle stick-figure family portraits with dialogue boxes and funny quotes I recall.

I want to tell you how my grandmother used to slip twenty-dollar bills into my birthday cards but now gives me poems instead. I want to tell you how they always end rhyming "lots of love" with "God's blessings from above."

I want to tell you how my grandmother's handwriting is the same as my wife's grandmother's handwriting and how, when my wife first saw a birthday card magnetized to the fridge in my dorm room, she wanted to cry. I want to tell you how, the week before we started dating, my wife had been in Paris with school friends and gotten a call that her grandmother died in her sleep.

I want to tell you how much I should cherish these cards, how sometimes I find them in boxes or drawers when moving and take a break to read them. I want my wife and I to carry these cards with us wherever we move.

I want copies of my grandmother's grocery lists to teach my daughter proper cursive. I want my daughter to have her grandmothers' handwriting, both my mother's and my wife's. I want my daughter to have her mother's looks. I want my son to have his father's handwriting. I want my son to have his mother's looks. I want my father to help me teach my children to fish, to make pyramids of charcoal, to tell the story of how their great-grandfather kept the lake from disappearing.

I want my mother-in-law to teach my children to paint and make jewelry. I want my father-in-law to take them for drives in convertible sports cars.

I want my wife and I to be proud of our children.

I want to watch our children gut trout with steak knives and garden hoses.

I want our children to have nothing but favorites.

I want my mother to teach the children their manners. I want to take the children shopping for sandals and rent them old VHS tapes. I want my mother to teach me her pork enchiladas and stroganoff. I want my grandmother to teach me her meatballs and mashed potatoes. I want to clean the wooden gutters of my grandmother's house with a gloved hand and proper screwdriver. I want to string Christmas lights on that old house with my children holding the ladder.

I want to throw pinecones at trees. I want to break sticks over my knee. I want to turn over rocks and look at the bugs.

I want to fly a lure-shaped kite from a boat in a fishing hole and tell the kids, This is how you fish for a jumper.

I want the earth to stop spinning so we can live in
constant dawn.

I want to row across an ocean and find, in the middle out
there, something like the heaven where my grandfather
lives. I want to take my wife there to meet him, our children there to visit. I want to bring him this book and say,
I wrote this for you.

I want bioluminescent flowers at that place in the ocean.
I want them to open at night and glow there beneath us. I
want magnolia trees to rise from the depths and brighten
in darkness. I want to breathe in the air and listen to the
waves lap against our boat. I want music in the trees,
something beautiful I've never heard before, like what our
prayers might sound like to god.

I want beauty, unencumbered, and joy.

I want with this day, my daily bread.

I want

I want to wake early on weekend mornings and make omelets full of peppers and mushrooms and seasonings. I want to make pancakes and French toast, croque madames and monsieurs. I want to take a French cooking course. I want to retake French in high school. I want to learn better knife skills. I want to dice an onion in under thirty seconds without tearing. I want to juggle chef's knives while singing out Good morning! to my waking family in different languages.

I want to invent a better coffee pot. I want to grow coffee beans in the yard. I want to wake earlier in the mornings and watch the sunrise. I want cooped chickens and fresh eggs. I want to worry about foxes sneaking stealthily from The Woods.

I want to tell you about the big empty lot across the street from the house I grew up in, where now there are two houses, both bigger and with newer paint jobs and professional lawns. I want to tell you how the neighbor boy and I used to pick blackberries from the bushes that grew there before the new neighbors cleared them out. I want to tell you how our mothers baked pies and made jam and how we'd sell their jams and pies on the sides of busier streets like we were a lemonade stand.

I want to tell you how we used to play war in that lot, in The Woods, how we'd make bows and arrows from whittled sticks and tree limbs and shoot at each other or at pop cans we'd line up on flat rocks.

I want to tell you about the pocketknives we both got for our thirteenth birthdays one year, his red and mine blue, and how he got his first because his birthday was three weeks before mine. I want to tell you how even though I knew I was getting a knife too, for those three weeks I was jealous and hated him as only a twelve-year-old boy can hate another, and how for those three weeks the weapons he whittled were so much better than mine because he had a sharpened red pocket knife to whittle with, and I had only an old steak knife. I want to tell you how, because he didn't share the red knife, our games of war then became more real, more fierce, and for those few weeks we stopped playing games and had real fights. I want to tell you how I took that red knife finally, when his mother called him to help her bring in the groceries, and for those few minutes I had the power to make better weapons too, and I did, a sharp and heavy arrow like a spear, and when he came back outside he was crying because he'd realized I'd taken his knife, and even though I put the red knife back on the rock where he'd left it, it was only after I aimed my brand new arrow right at his chest and said, Go ahead, it's right there, I left it for you. I want to tell you how he took it and ran, still crying, and how, even though I didn't fire, I just stood there in the woods alone and started crying too, because I knew a couple days later I would unwrap my own blue knife and be sad, because then we would both have these more powerful knives, and we would both know, looking at each other across all that wrapping paper and birthday cake, that we couldn't play war anymore.

I want

I want to slice half a finger and have it grow back. I want
to cook with oil and make a giant fireball above the stove.
I want burn scars from cooking. I want to singe off my
eyebrows and look in the mirror. I want to shave my head.
I want to grow a full beard. I want my hair to go gray and
grow long and flowy.

I want to plant nail clippings in a flowerbed and see if they
bloom with polish the color of petals. I want to spend a
day planting seeds and watering roses. I want to pick wild
blackberries with my children and teach them to
bake a pie.

I want to teach my children the wildness of wilderness, the
wildness of creation. I want to pass on my passions. I want
my children not to want for anything.

I want to take my father to Finland to visit the city of
Riippi in the Teuva region. I want to take my children to
Finland and the city of Riippi in the Teuva region. I want
to walk with them through a field and say, This is where
your grandfather once tended reindeer.

I want my children to love their family.

I want my children to look confused when their friends tell
them how much they hate their parents.

I want my children's friends to say how cool my wife
and I are.

I want my children to do what they love. I want them to go to college. I want them to love books.

I want my children to admire their mother and father for the lives that we're living.

I want to walk along springtime sidewalks in New York City and have our children say how much the flowering trees bursting from the grey pavement look like whale spouts.

I want our children to love the morning blossoms of a magnolia.

I want our children to meet the old woman making dinner in the window of the brownstone on 22nd Street. I want her to invite us in for bread and juice, to let my children run up and down her stairs playing hide and seek while she shares with my wife and me her life's fictions and truths.

I want our children to look at the sky from the roof of that brownstone and say how much they wish they could fly. I want our children to be able to close their eyes and imagine what it would be like to fly, and I want imagination to be enough. I want our children to have strong imaginations, to fly magic carpets in their minds, to see what's possible just by sitting at a window in the rain.

I want our children to have imaginary friends who are good influences. I want their imaginary friends to tell jokes that our children share. I want them to be funny.

I want a stronger imagination. I want my dreams to come

true. I want to not dream so much. I want to not want what can only happen in dreams. I want to be invited to an award show for some kind of lifetime achievement. I want to give a speech on international television so that I can thank everyone I love for everything they are. I want to not care about awards.

I want to win an international literature award of great merit. I want fame and great fortune.

I want to not look forward to the weekends. I want to sail around the world with only my wife and some books and a hot plate. I want to go back to Turkey. I want to go back to Cappadocia where my wife and I took a hot air balloon ride at sunrise. I want to go back to that painted chapel buried in the cave none of the tour groups visited. I want to go back to that little Florentine pizza place where my wife and I shared a bottle of wine for breakfast and practiced poor Italian for hours. I want to go back to Paris and read a great novel in its entirety beneath the Pont Neuf while snow falls along the Seine. I want to relive the day I turned 21 and did that. I want to learn everything by memory. I want to recite great novels by heart. I want to recite all things by heart.

I want to learn without forgetting and to remember as I please.

I want to have written that last sentence earlier in this book—it's what I've been trying to get at.

I want to rewrite my memory. I want to not edit this. I want to relive my favorite memories as I remember them now, but with improvements. I want to remember a fishing trip catching sharks that never happened. I want to remember climbing Mount Rainier. I want to make things happen just by choosing to remember them.

I want to remember snorkeling in a coral reef the color of magnolia with sea turtles and starfish smiling all about me.

I want to spend a day seeing everything a fish sees, especially a spawning salmon or a South African shark.

I want to live in an aquarium.

I want to live in the desert.

I want to live in The Woods.

I want to live on top of a mountain.

I want to live in a cave.

I want to live in a pyramid, or on top of one.

I want to live in a hot air balloon.

I want to live in the Eiffel Tower.

I want to live in a tree house.

I want to live in a glass submarine.

I want to live in the house next door to the house I grew up in.

I want to be my own neighbor.

I want to live in that brownstone on 22nd Street with the
magnolia out front and the basil plants in the window and
all that exposed brick.

I want to live in outer space and point to all the
places I'd like to live.

I want to sit on a satellite and sing. I want to see another
planet up close. I want to walk on the moon. I want to
golf on the moon.

I want to write poetry in the surface of the moon with a
finger so that someday a child can gaze through a telescope
and read what I wrote there. I want that child
to read and say, Oh.

I want to write something with enough heart to carry it to
the surface of the moon. I want what I want so much
I can't stand it.

I want gratitude. I want kindness. I want peace. I want
heart and heart and heart.

I want to be better at writing thank you notes. I want to
design grandfatherly jewelry, like pocket watches and cuf-
flinks and tie clips. I want to dress better. I want better
posture. I want refinement and poise.

I want to write a play in iambic tetrameter. I want to dig a
hole to China. I want to build a tree fort for my children.

I want to write a Broadway musical about quails or some
other kind of beautiful bird.

I want to paint pictures of beautiful blooming magnolias
with quails living in them.

I want my musical to be funny without being crude, and I
want to use fewer curse words, especially fuck.

I want to be admired by my coworkers. I want to carry myself well in social situations. I want to be a more functional
introvert. I want an apartment in which to hold dinner parties. I want the kind of friends I'd be excited to invite over
for dinner parties. I want to have lively, voluminous laughter and conversations about art and theater and music.

I want to play piano by ear. I want perfect pitch. I want a
baby grand piano in a living room. I want a terrace over-
looking a park. I want a player piano next to the baby
grand. I want it to play all of the songs we've
forgotten we loved.

I want to know what songs were sung to sing me
to sleep as a baby.

I want to know what songs I'll sing to a baby of my own.
I want to knit a baby blanket while humming in a rocking
chair. I want to practice singing softly.

I want

I want to tell you about my grandmother, ninety-one-years-old now, and living alone at the lake house. I want to tell you how she used to make up songs for the grandchildren to sing on holidays. I want to sing for you "Happy Lake House Holiday" and her Easter-altered version of "Silent Night."

I want to tell you how she always has her telephone on speaker mode, how its handset is louder than a television.

I want you to understand how, if you were to call my grandmother on her birthday or wedding anniversary to say something nice, like congratulations or happy birthday, she would say thank you and then get off the phone as fast as possible, because she thinks the phone call is costing you a lot of money, and she can't really hear what you're saying anyway, I want you to know, though, that she does really appreciate the call. I want to tell you how, after you called her for one of those short conversations, she'd then call everyone else in the family to let them know how nice it was of you to call.

I want to know how often she mistakes a noise on the television for the phone ringing.

I want to tell you about the time my grandmother was hospitalized for dehydration. I want to tell you how, when the doctor asked her how much water she drank each day, she answered, Oh, a pot or two, depending on the weather. I want to tell you how we laughed when the doctor asked

what she meant by pot or two, and she said, Well, what do
you make your coffee in, a bedpan? I want you to understand that never in my life can I remember seeing my
grandmother drinking a plain glass of water, even after my
grandfather dug a well and they stopped filling jugs from
our garden hose.

I want to tell you how my grandmother hates squirrels and
loves raccoons. I want to tell you how she loves seagulls
and hates hummingbirds. I want to tell you how she loved
her grandchildren but hates the neighbors'. I want to tell
you about her hernia, how she got it trying to lift a garbage
can full of rain water, and how all that rain
knocked her over.

I want to tell you about the dead mouse she left in the
kitchen overnight, as a warning to others.

I want to tell you about the time she stayed at the kitchen
window all night with a camera, hoping to catch a neighbor boy stealing gravel from her driveway.

I want to tell you how she insists that the green-headed
mallards are actually female, because they're prettier than
the brown.

I want to tell you about the bear she chased out of her
yard with a broom, and how when we told her it probably
wasn't a good idea for her to go outside after seeing a bear
through the window, she said, Well it was just so cute—I
would have shot it if it weren't.

I want to tell you about her Santa Claus collection, seventy
years since the first ceramic was bought at a drug store in

Tacoma. I want to tell you how, when you climb through
her attic and stoop in search of Christmas lights, the tiny
Santas are the first thing you see, some draped in sheets
like ghosts, others posed like murderous elves in hiding. I
want to tell you about the time I hid behind the battery-
powered big one and how I turned it on as my father
climbed up looking for me. I want to have gotten
his scream on tape.

I want to tell you about my grandmother's mashed potatoes, half a stick of butter for every spud. I want to tell
you how she smiles when she can't hear you, how she
listens when you ask her to, or at least tries.

I want to tell you about the time she put a small carton
of yogurt in her purse at the grocery store, because her
cart was full, and then forgot to pay for it. I want to tell
you how she came back later that evening to apologize
and how the manager told her not to worry about it, to
consider the yogurt a gift. I want to tell you how, when she
told me this story over coffee, she leaned in as if to tell a
secret, then whispered, I think he had a thing for me.

I want to sit with you on the shore of a lake and tell you
all her stories. I want you to remember my grandmother
with love, as I do, even if you've never met her.

I want to know if the stories about the mice and bears and
neighbor thieves were true or just stories she made up
for our benefit.

I want you to understand that it's entirely plausible that my
grandmother made up all these stories.

I want you to understand it's entirely possible
she never existed.

I want you to understand how much I love hearing her
tell these stories.

I want to know what I don't know about her.

I want to know what she wanted and never got.

I want

I want to know if I will eulogize my grandmother.

I want to have time to prepare. I want to go through several drafts. I want to do it well, when it happens, if it happens. I want to get it right.

I want to know how long I still have to prepare. I want it to be a long time.

I want to say, when it happens, that what I'll miss most about her are the chats at the lake house kitchen table over coffee. I want to say how she never told me much in those chats I hadn't already heard from my parents or sister—her stories spread quickly through the telephone lines—but it was nice just to sit there with her, sipping her weak and too-hot coffee, inquiring if she'd seen any bears lately.

I want to tell you about the first time my grandmother and grandfather saw each other, when she was at a city park in Tacoma, picnicking with a friend, and they were listening to a radio. I want to tell you how a young and handsome soldier carrying a suitcase walked up to my grandmother to introduce himself. I want to tell you how my grandmother says she didn't want to talk to him, how she thought he was suspicious, but it was her friend who thought he was handsome and invited my grandfather to share their sandwiches. I want to tell you how, when he sat down and opened the suitcase, there was a sardine and egg sandwich inside, a thermos of coffee he offered to share.

I want to know what radio program my grandmother and her friend were listening to that got my grandfather's attention, because my grandmother can never remember. I want to know if my grandfather would remember if he were still alive to be asked.

I want to have been hiding in a tree high above the rose bushes, watching my grandparents and the sprouting magnolias below.

I want to tell you how, when I was a junior in college on the east coast and my father called to tell me my grandfather had died, he wasn't crying, but he was trying hard not to. I want to tell you how I was very conscious of that call being a moment I would remember. I want to tell you how what I remember now of the moment is not sadness, but rather a kind of memory of future remembering, a weird narcissism or self-consciousness, a kind of repeating loop, like a skipping record. I want to know what scientists call that.

I want to tell you how, when I was a pallbearer alongside my cousins, I wanted to let myself feel all the emotions of loss and love that I thought a person should feel at a family funeral. I want to confess that while we were carrying the giant coffin across the wet grass to his grave, all I could think was Don't Slip, Don't Drop It, Don't Slip, Don't Drop It, Don't Slip. I want you to understand, it was so much heavier than I expected.

I want to be better at expectations.

I want to have that day to do over, to really make it count. I want the grass to be dry and my hands to be less sweaty.

I want the sun to peak out of the clouds just enough to spotlight our path. I want a strong grip and a lighter coffin. I want it to be sixty-five degrees and the sunlight bright ahead of me so that I can see everything and take it all in.

I want to confess I don't remember what the weather was like, just that the grass was wet and I was sweating and uncomfortable in a musted suit.

I want to be able to wear a black zippered sweatshirt and jeans and sneakers every day. I want it to be sixty-five degrees every day. I want to wear jeans and a sweatshirt to weddings and funerals and have no one notice that I'm not wearing a suit. I want that to be appropriate. I want that to be my superpower, which I don't think is too much to ask.

I want to not ever have to wear a suit again.

I want to not ever have to speak at a funeral unprepared, but I want to give an eloquent eulogy for someone dearly loved by many.

I want to have given my grandfather a great eulogy instead of just sitting and sweating in a pew.

I want you to understand how guilty I feel sometimes just for being alive.

I want to know what soldiers died who would have lived better lives than I have. I want to know what college students have surrendered and swallowed the pills and not been saved. I want to know what I can do to save them. I want to know if they want to be saved. I want to know if, for some suicides, death really is the better the option, the

path we would all choose in their situation, like euthanasia
for the terminally ill, or a medieval traitor who chooses
decapitation over being disemboweled.

I want to know what I ever did to deserve a good life.

I want to know if it's just me, or if you ever wonder
that about yourself.

I want to not be alone in this.

I want

I want to know what it's like to fight in a modern war.

I want to feel as if I've earned the right to a happy life. I want to feel as though I've fought for it and deserve it.

I want to know what it was like to fight in the Civil War. I want to go back in time and watch a battle invisibly from a hot air balloon, just above the reach of cannon fire.

I want

I want to make more out of whatever it is I've been given.

I want to visit Ancient Rome with my wife, invisibly, and walk about. I want to visit Renaissance Florence invisibly and walk about. I want to watch Michelangelo stare down a block of marble. I want to watch Michelangelo polish the last bit of his David and step back to admire his work. I want to know if he was happy with it. I want to touch the cheek of the David, gently, as Michelangelo might have done.

I want to know if Michelangelo did all the sculpting himself or if he had many assistants. I want to meet the Pope and ask if he felt closer to God the moment the smoke went up declaring him Pope. I want to say a rosary with the Pope. I want to play a game of table tennis with the Pope. I want to meet the assistant who cleans the glass on the Pope Mobile. I want to know if the cleaning solution is blessed. I want to know if the toilet water in the Vatican is blessed. I want to beat the Pope in a game of checkers, just so I can say, King me.

I want to know what it feels like to be crucified. I want to know what it feels like to be disemboweled and beheaded.

I want to fire a bow and arrow. I want to watch a band of Apaches in the nineteenth century firing their bows and arrows from horseback and shouting. I want to know what it smells like from the back of a horse, riding hard and sweating through the plains.

I want to know if one person can carve a totem pole, or if
it takes many assistants.

I want to run with the bison. I want to run with the bulls. I
want to run a marathon. I want to swim, run,
and bike a triathlon.

I want to tell you about the sea turtle my wife and I saw
swimming through coral like a flying elephant or dumb
kind of dinosaur, which I suppose it was, or could have
been. I want to relive the time of the dinosaurs. I want to
feel the humidity of tyrannosaur breath and slide down the
neck of a brachiosaurus. I want to ride a rhino. I want to
sprint between the legs of a giraffe. I want a safari in my
backyard. I want an aquarium beneath my floorboards, a
porthole for a window, starfish in the window boxes
and orca in the distance.

I want to walk invisibly through a pride of sleeping lions. I
want to run invisibly with a herd of gazelles.

I want to live in a castle for a week. I want to write entirely
on shreds of parchment with peacock feather pens and in-
digo inks by the faint light of dirty candles. I want to leave
bike tire skid marks down the length of a driveway.

I want to break into a prison and lift weights. I want to fish
in a pond with a stick and a shoelace and a pill bottle or
seedling for a bobber.

I want to take one big dip of chewing tobacco and ride on
a roller coaster alone.

I want to skydive strapped to my wife. I want to pop wheelies for distance on a tandem bike. I want to throw a tantrum in a grocery store and throw plums at the checkers.

I want to know if there are museum people responsible for dusting the David and, since there must be, what they use for the dusting. I want to know if it's just one person responsible for that or if it's a whole team polishing at the same time. I want to know if that looks like a strange orgy.

I want to stand strong as a statue on the seashore and experience a hurricane. I want to be chased by a raging forest fire. I want to evacuate in the wake of lahar. I want to snorkel through a swamp. I want to breathe underwater.

I want to be able to swim in air, almost like flying but not quite. I want to conduct a magnificent orchestra while wearing jeans and a sweatshirt.

I want to visit the ancient place where David fought Goliath and watch the fight invisibly. I want to know if David's slung stone still exists in a pile somewhere or if it's eroded to dust. I want to visit all the ancient times and walk about invisibly.

I want to know if wars ever really end or if it's just that certain people say they do.

I want my wife and I to vacation through time. I want us to visit Egypt during the building of the pyramids but still be able to stay at the Four Seasons. I want us to visit King Arthur's court but still be able to stay at the Soho House. I want us to walk invisibly through the fires at Dresden untouched. I want us to turn invisible at will.

I want us to release black helium balloons from the bottom of the Hudson River and stand on the roof of that brown-stone on 22nd Street to watch them emerge and arise slimy and dripping with goo like chemical bombs in a slow-motion reverse.

I want, before we have children, for my wife and I to share every great adventure.

I want us to undo damage. I want us to undo destruction. I want us to deconstruct destruction.

I want us to never stop wanting us.

I want to tell you how we will be having children soon, and how I am terrified by how much I still don't know, but I do want to tell you what I do know—that a person must figure out what it is they want before they can truly know how to live. I want to tell you what I've learned, or think I have, that the only way to really figure out what you want your life to be is to never stop wanting more of it.

Part Two

I want

I want to tell you what my grandfather said to me the last time I saw him alive.

I want to tell you how, when he was dying, he was dying of Parkinson's disease, and so the closer his body got to giving out, the more it shook in protest. I want to tell you how, towards the very end of it, my grandmother said he started seeing things on the walls. I want to tell you how he built those lake house walls with his bare hands and how now they were attacking him.

I want to tell you how, when he had to stay in a hospital bed, my grandmother had him moved from the bedroom they'd shared for forty years into one closer to the front door, so it would be easier for the emergency people to reach him when something happened.

I want to tell you how my father and I carried a small bed into that room for my grandmother to sleep in, so she could be there when he woke screaming at night.

I want to tell you how the small bed we moved into that room was the same bed I used to sleep in when I stayed over as a kid. I want to tell you how the blanket my grandmother would wrap herself in as an old woman was the same blanket I had been wrapped in as a boy.

I want to tell you how, the summer I was eighteen and about to leave for college on the east coast, my grandmother went on a trip to Reno with some of her friends. I

want to tell you how my grandfather had been doing better
the past couple months, and how very tired my grandmother was, and how much she needed a break, and how I
knew this might be the last time I'd have a chance to spend
time alone with my grandfather.

I want to tell you how he wasn't supposed to drink coffee,
but he asked for it and so I gave it to him.

I want to tell you how he wasn't supposed to have sugar,
but he asked for cookies and so I gave him a whole plate.

I want to tell you how he wasn't supposed to have alcohol,
but he asked for schnapps and so that was the only drink
we ever had together, and we sipped those sweet snifters
while watching videos of old World Series, because he
liked to keep score, even after the tremors in his hands got
so bad he couldn't hold a pencil.

I want to tell you how, when he woke in the middle of the
night, he said he saw spiders crawling out of the walls, and
I didn't know what to do but slap at what I couldn't see.
I want to explain to you what it felt like when he pointed
his shaky hands around the room at the spiders breaking
through, saying, There, there, there, and how I crushed
them beneath my palm each time, scrambling, shouting
back, Don't worry, don't worry, I've got you.

I want to tell you how I sat awake next to him for a long
while to make sure he was sleeping, his jaw and hands
still shaking. I want to tell you how I thought I'd have to
change the sheets but then remembered the catheter.

I want to tell you how my grandmother was only gone two

nights, but both nights he woke up seeing spiders, and
both nights I killed them all.

I want to know what would have happened if he had seen
something other than spiders, something too big for me to
kill with my bare hands.

I want to tell you how, the morning before my grandmother got home, I was making coffee in the kitchen when I
heard him calling out for my grandmother. I want to tell
you how, when I came into the room saying, No grandpa,
it's me, grandma will be back tonight, he said, Oh! Hi
Billy!, and I said, No, grandpa, I'm Joe, Billy's son,
and then he smiled and said, your Joey's a good boy, Billy,
and closed his eyes.

I want to tell you how he muttered, You made a good son,
Billy, and fell asleep.

I want to tell you how, when I was a little kid visiting the
lake house, my grandfather would take me out to the dock
and pick me up and throw me as far as he could, and I
would spread my arms wide, and he would laugh loud, and
it was like I was flying high over the water, climbing farther
and farther away.

I want to tell you how he taught me to cartwheel and
taught me to sing.

I want to tell you how we drank beers together and looked
out at the lake and he told me the story of the time he
pounded a nail into a cedar tree with his bare hand.

I want to tell you that I talked to him once more before he

died, but I didn't. I want to tell the truth, and the truth is
he was still asleep when my grandmother got home, and
I left for college a few weeks later, which is where I was
when my father called to let me know that my grandfather
had died in the middle of the night

I want to know why he couldn't say that my grandfather
died in his sleep. I want to know if maybe he was awake
for it, if that's why.

I want to know if he woke in the middle of the night and
my grandmother wasn't able to keep the spiders away. I
want to know if he died screaming or in pain.

I want him to have died in his sleep.

I want it to be just that language is vague sometimes.

I want it to be just that when my father said, Middle of the
night, he meant, In his sleep, and I'm just over-thinking it.

I want

I want to tell you about the time I was five and my mother lost me in the supermarket, or I lost her, and instead of finding an adult who worked there like I was supposed to, I stole a donut from its box and sat on the floor, hiding and licking maple-sticky fingers.

I want to tell you how I once hid in the attic for most of a Saturday, reading comics beside the Santas, and how no one noticed, or at least didn't comment, but only asked me if I had a nice day when I came down for dinner.

I want to tell you how it made me feel like an adult to know I could do what I wanted.

I want to tell you how it made me feel like if I went away my family might never know.

I want to know what we ate for dinner. I want to know if I was happy or sad. I want to know if they knew I'd been hiding.

I want to know what they're all doing right now, right this second. I want to know if they ever raise a glass and toast to their son who moved so far away, if they wonder why I left and if it had anything to do with them.

I want to know if my mother remembers that time in the supermarket, because all I remember is the story of it, the version she told me.

I want to know if they ever get tired of the same grocery stores and streets. I want to know if they ever wish they'd left, too, like I did.

I want to tell you about the time I skipped school and just got on the highway and drove and drove and drove, and after having lunch somewhere south of Portland I came home at the regular time, and nobody ever knew.

I want to say that returning home from Oregon was the moment I knew I would leave, or that I knew I wanted to do something real with my life. I want to have started *doing* at that moment, but what I've done, really, is *want*.

I want

I want a library like those in great English manors, com-
plete with a ladder-track and leatherback chairs like
thrones. I want a house capable of housing tapestries. I
want a home where a tapestry would not seem absurd. I
want a coat of arms, a magnolia etched in coarse thread
and profiled pack-mules to frame it. I want a leather jacket
with a fur-trimmed collar. I want to stand at the bow of a
boat in my jacket, the fur brushing against my neck
in the sea wind.

I want to know what it was like on the Titanic, before the
crash, and after.

I want to tell you the story of how my grandmother's
mother was supposed to be on the Titanic, how she sup-
posedly had a ticket but never used it, how she was fash-
ionably late for the departure.

I want the reason to be that she met her future husband
and lost track of time. I want this to be a romantic story. I
want to write a romance.

I want to know if it's true that she had a ticket, or if it's
just a family rumor that got started and still hasn't stopped.

I want to know what happened to that ticket
she never used.

I want to frame that ticket on my wall and pass it down as
an heirloom, a reminder of the importance of romance

in our lives.

I want to know what it's like to be a movie star, someone
pretending to fall in love.

I want to know what it's like to float on a life raft and
watch a ship sink.

I want to swim in the middle of the ocean and know I am
a thousand miles away from any land. I want to scream at
the top of my lungs while treading water mid-Atlantic.

I want to ride on the back of an albatross from one distant
island to the next. I want to sit alone on a tiny island with
a single palm tree. I want to wish for five books and five
films. I want to know, in that situation, trapped on a desert
island, if favorite books or films would offer any solace or
just be a painful reminder of what I've lost.

I want a blank book to fill up with prayers. I want a blank
book to fill up with memories to relive. I want a blank
book to fill up with fictions.

I want all my memories on five videotapes.

I want to spend my desert-island time reliving all the good
moments that led up to it. I want to make new memories
by stepping out often for swims.

I want to float on my back, gaze up at the stars, and
remember that summer evening driving eastward through
Montana with a best friend, when the sunset in the rear-
view was too much orange to let pass, and we had to pull
over to smoke and to stare.

I want to remember what we said right then.

I want to remember what we said the rocks looked like.

I want to remember what music we listened to just after.

I want to relive driving through North Dakota at night, when we turned off the headlights to look at the stars that were glowing like the millions of distant suns that they are.

I want to remember when it was that someone first told me most stars we see are actually dead, that they died long ago, it's just that the light hasn't gone out yet.

I want to camp for several days on a rock in Western Montana and stare at the stars and write down whatever stray thoughts occur to me.

I want to fill five notebooks and put them in bottles and send them out to sea for anyone trapped on an island.

I want to know how many stars there are that we don't see, even though it's a number that's probably too high to really understand.

I want to spend a day as a chaff of wheat somewhere in Nebraska or Oklahoma or Kansas. I want to paint a road bright yellow with black stripes.

I want to know how many of the stars we see are long dead.

I want to know how long it'll be after I die before anyone

knows. I want to know if I'll see spiders attacking first. I want to know who, if anyone, will be there to save me.

I want to know how I look in videotapes, how I look in other people's memories. I want to know whether I am a bustling hearth of life or just an island.

I want

I want to be less sweaty so as to be more comfortable in
dress clothes.

I want to understand why I sweat so much when I'm under
stress. I want to be able to unstress myself at will.

I want to know if maybe beta-blockers would help me. I
want to not be embarrassed to ask my doctor for something to help with my sweating. I want to know if this
runs in the family.

I want to tell you how, if I were telling you a story right
now at a dinner party, especially a fancy dinner party with
fancy cocktails and fancy piano music, I would pay very
close attention to your eyes, to see if you notice the stains
growing underneath my arms. I want you to understand
that there's nothing I can do about it, that as soon as I fo-
cus on the sweating, it gets even worse, and that even right
now, writing this in my bedroom, I can feel the moistening
and worsening of it.

I want to know how sweaty I would be alone on a desert
island. I want to know if it's more the embarrassment that
causes the sweat, and so being alone on a hot beach in the
middle of the ocean would be less sweaty than a winter
workday in Manhattan.

I want a cure for embarrassment. I want a cure for anxiety.
I want a cure for stress.
I want to not feel such anxiety about imagined things like

this that don't matter, what thoughts I've made up and hyperbolized, but I can't help but feel how I do, or help what I do, and so it must matter, I think, because even imagined spiders can scare the life out of you.

I want a relaxing beach house in the Hamptons where I'll serve fancy drinks and play fancy piano and wear thin, colorful shirts that never stain.

I want to learn to unstress myself through productivity.

I want to build a piano from scratch and sing for no reason at all.

I want to build a house in Chelsea with a Mediterranean beach as its backyard and a grove of magnolias as its front. I want to fall asleep listening to the waves. I want to wake hearing waves surrounding us, lapping the roots of our front yard, turning our great house into an island.

I want to learn to surf, to ride the waves between the magnolia trunks. I want to dive deep into the water and look up at blurry, floating petals.

I want to watch you surf over me. I want to rise and call out to you, see you turn on your board, smile and spill into the sea.

I want us to swim together amongst the tree trunks and falling petals, the blues and the greens and the magnolia, yellow sunlight warming the water with thick rays. I want to call out to you and have you be my wife.

I want you to know you are the only one who relaxes me.

I want us to swim together until we're too tired to float, and then paddle exhaustedly back to our front door. I want us to spend every weekend like this. I want us to spend our lives like this. I want us to always call out to one another. I want us to relive this over and over throughout the week. I want our children to call us on weekends and ask, How was your morning surf? as we sip our tea and espresso, dripping and exhausted in our kitchen, at our island, smelling of salt and licking our lips and smiling.

I want

I want our children to telephone my wife and me more
often than I call my parents.

I want better cellular reception. I want an espresso ma-
chine. I want espresso to be good for me. I want health to
be delicious. I want all that is delicious to be good for me
and all that is disgusting to be good for me. I want more
and better health in general. I want more life in general. I
want more love in general.

I want a private restaurant with a glistening kitchen where
I can make my favorite dishes for all my friends. I want a
self-filling refrigerator and self-cleaning pans and pots that
never stain. I want a paring knife that never dulls. I want to
be better at handling knives. I want to witness a medieval
swordfight, invisibly. I want to know what it's like to wear a
suit of armor. I want to know what it's like to ride a horse
through the English countryside while wearing
a suit of armor.

I want to learn more about mixology. I want to invent
a drink to serve at black tie dinner parties. I want better
anecdotes and dry underarms.

I want to carry a piano to a desert island beach at very low
tide and play soft chords as the water moves and flows in
around me.

I want to float away on the piano top, singing, waiting for
stars and my voice to give out.

I want

I want to paint a stop sign green and call it art, just for laughs. I want to make art sometimes just for the fun of it. I want more people to understand that that's all art is sometimes, just fun, and that's okay, that's good, at least as far as I want it to be. I want to remind you that all of this is fiction, and I'm just making it up as I go along.

I want artists to take their art seriously, but not so seriously that it stops being fun.

I want to open an art gallery that is also a library, and I want to open a coffee shop that is also a bar and a sandwich shop, all in one room, in one building, like the one I saw in Berlin. I want to backpack across Europe to get more ideas, and I want to drive across Europe, or bike across Europe, all of it, stopping at every vineyard and café along the way to learn about cheeses. I want to carry baguettes and wine in the basket of a bike. I want to learn the word for *cheese monger* in every European language. I want to write the terms into a kind of list poem, and I want to nap on the edge of all the bridges in Prague. I want to speak to a crowd on a ferry in Sweden and read my list poem about cheeses at Speaker's Corner in Hyde Park. I want to invite you to my new gallery that is also a library, which is next to my coffee shop that is also a bar that serves sandwiches with pink-purple petals for garnish.

I want you to know that I love you for reading this, for listening.

I want you to know how much it means to me that you are reading this.

I want you to know I am putting my whole heart into this but that I am also having fun. I want you to help me know the limits of my heart, how far it can go and how much it can want. I want to know if it will ever stop, this wanting and desiring and yearning, but I know someday it will, it has to, because a heart just stops beating, always, just stops, like a thud.

I want to eat less red meat and drink less dark liquor. I want to eat shepherd's pie with black pints on a rainy Sunday in Galway. I want to eat haggis in Scotland. I want to learn to bake bread in Sicily. I want to pick lemons in Greece. I want to read poetry in an English meadow beside a stranger doing the same.

I want to shear sheep. I want to knit sweaters. I want to give scarves as gifts to all my friends. I want to knit myself an orange scarf. I want to knit matching red and green holiday sweaters for my family. I want to frame the picture of us in those sweaters and hang it above a mantel. I want to reread every book I've ever read, especially those I didn't care for, and I want to care for those books now, especially the good bits I didn't quite understand, or wasn't old enough to understand. I want to recognize the metaphors and rhythms, the parataxis and poesy. I want to know how much all this reading has changed me. I want to know what I'd have been like if my parents had made me read less or hadn't encouraged me toward books. I want to have written it down. I want to have kept a journal then, like I keep notebooks now.

I want to relive by way of reading, especially those moments I remember now sadly, to see how and if they changed me for the better.

I want to know what my parents were like as children, as teens, at my age now.

I want to follow my parents invisibly to a party in college. I want to follow my parents invisibly the day they brought my home from the hospital.

I want to know what it would have been like to meet my wife in high school. I want to know what it would have been like to take my wife to prom. I want to have taken my wife to football games and mixers. I want to take my wife dancing. I want us to dance on the deck of a riverboat or along a waterfront promenade. I want us to dance in the rain of an empty city street at midnight. I want us to float above Paris cobblestones, toes barely touching, like ballerinas, spotlit by the moon our bodies lifted by an umbrella caught and carried in heavy wind.

I want to write whole operas about what I feel when I'm holding my wife's hand beside a blooming magnolia.

I want some kind of reassurance that what I'm doing in life is all right. I want some kind of reassurance that I am not wasting my time in writing down even my most absurd wantings, like that I want to be a mouse riding in an upside down umbrella down river rapids or that I want to ride a bicycle that flies itself with mechanical wings.

I want to grow very small and ride on the back of a spider as it weaves its web, for no reason other than I had the idea and it seems like a lovely, fun, and artistic thing to do.

I want

I want to ride a bicycle on the moon.

I want to ride a bicycle down a ski slope in summer time. I want to ride a bicycle down a ski slope in winter and take it off a mighty jump.

I want to start a snowball fight in a crowded football stadium. I want snow to fall bright orange once a year, on a blanket of already-fallen white.

I want to throw a bright orange snowball across a bright blue sky from the top of an even brighter cotton-white mountain.

I want to be ice fishing on an enormous lake alone when the snow starts to fall, and I want to watch it build up on the ice like petals of some strange tropical flower, and then I want to paint it.

I want

I want us, my wife and our children and me, to live on a houseboat for a summer.

I want us to sail the houseboat down the Mississippi River like a travelling desert island, reading to each other and writing stories for each other and drinking iced tea in the evenings while a New Orleans jazz band plays from a raft floating nearby. I want the kids to go to bed as my wife and I listen deep into the dark hours, when we sip gimlets and juleps and slap at mosquito swarms.

I want to spend the early hours of morning translating our family stories into French and Hungarian and Finnish. I want to rock in a rocking chair on the porch of a travelling island and write letters to whomever we love back home.

I want us to keep the boat going out the mouth of the Delta, but only after we stop to play blues on a porch somewhere in Baton Rouge. I want us to see the old jazz clubs of the fifties as they were at their best. I want us to hear the old crooners unamplified. I want to walk invisibly to the crossroads with aspiring blues guitarists and hear them pray to the devil for inhuman skills. I want a personal bugle reveille the morning after, and then I want to sail across the ocean in a clipper ship, the wind our only propulsion.

I want to watch my son climb into the rigging and spot whales from the crow's nest. I want to walk along the bottom of the sea with my daughter and have her tell me

about something she read in a book. I want us to hike the
colorful cliff towns of the Mediterranean. I want bottles
full of blank notebooks to wash up on the shore. I want to
learn how to draw and to do it every day.

I want our children to write us stories and read them
aloud before bedtime.

I want us to fly out to sea in a helicopter and see a spectac-
ular view of an island no one before us ever knew existed.

I want

I want to tell you about Jenns.

I want to tell you how Jenns was a friend of mine in high school on the football team.

I want to tell you how, when we really became friends, it was at our initiation into the team. I want to tell you how we'd both made varsity our first year and so had to be held down by a mob in a senior's garage while a 350-pounder called Gator shaved our heads with a single-blade razor and garden hose.

I want you to understand how happy we were, blue-headed and shivering with blood and hose water dripping down our faces.

I want to tell you how Gator laughed when he poured alcohol over our cuts after and how we laughed with him and how bad it stung and how it didn't hurt at all.

I want to tell you how, when Jenns and I saw each other in the school parking lot the next morning, we both had bandages on our heads, and how we were called into the principal's office together to confirm that we had asked Gator to shave our heads, that it was our own wanting and not any sort of hazing. I want to remember if we had to sign papers, but I can't.

I want to tell you how proud I felt to have Gator come up to me in the hall later and say, Lookin' good, brother.

I want you to understand how badly I'd wanted to be a part of this team my whole life leading up to it, how my father would take me to games and teach me positions and tell me how he had played football in high school, how much fun it had been for him, how good it was to have memories like that.

I want to tell you about the time a bunch of us from the team covered a cheerleader's house in toilet paper while she was away on vacation, and how even though Jenns was the fastest sprinter among us, he was the one who somehow got caught when the cops came. I want to tell you how he sat in the back of the cop car alone and lied, lied, lied, saying he had done the whole thing himself, when really there'd been close to thirty of us there. I want to tell you how even when the police called his mother, he lied then too, for us, his brothers. I want to tell you how even when they made him clean it up himself, right then at three in the morning, he kept lying. I want to tell you that when he got fined five hundred dollars, we all chipped in, and even then he wouldn't let us pay his share.

I want to know what kind of man Jenns would have grown up to be.

I want to explain that when I remember the team now, and all the games and championships we won, I think of Jenns before the rest.

I want to explain that when I think of loyalty and brotherhood now, I think of Jenns and soldiers like my grandfather.

I want to know what we talked about the last time we saw
each other, when I drove him home from practice, our hair
short and military. I want to know what we talked about
before I said, See you tomorrow, or Take it easy, or something silly like that. I want to know what we said before
we slapped hands and shook in the way sixteen-year-old
blood-brothers do, and before he disappeared inside. I
want to know why I didn't think it was strange he never invited me in. I want to know what the inside of that house
looked like. I want to know if there were pictures of family
on the walls, A-plus tests and postcards on the refrigerator,
letters from Texas where his soldier brother was stationed.
I want to know if there was anything Jenns could have said
on the drive home from practice that would have made me
think he might shoot himself in the head a few hours later,
which he did, with his soldier-brother's left-behind gun.

I want to know, still, if there's anything I could have said
that might have made a difference.

I want to tell you how the team retired Jenns' number, 4,
and how we markered JENNS 4 EVER on our shoe tape
and chalked it on our eye black for the next three seasons,
when those of us who knew him graduated. I want to
know if we won the game we still had to play a couple days
after, without Jenns, because I honestly don't remember
and I don't want to look it up. I want to know if we won,
but not if we lost.

I want to remember what the rest of us said to one
another that night.

I want to know if what the police officer told us is true,
that suicides often fire two shots because they're shaking

so badly with nerves, and they miss on the first try, or they
want to make sure the gun works.

I want to know how we knew that about the gun, who
would have told us that Jenns fired twice.

I want to know how many change their minds after
firing the first shot.

I want to have been in the room with him, invisibly. I want
to see how it happened, to see if he meant it.

I want to ask him if he would do it again if he could.

I want Jenns' family to know that we loved him.

I want Jenns to know how much his suicide changed me,
and it is horrible to write this, but I want him to know that
I am grateful.

I want to know how I would have turned out if he hadn't
died. I want to know what different kind of person I
would have become.

I want to know what was going through his head. I want to
understand it so well that I can move past
trying to understand it.

I want to stop writing about Jenns and his suicide now.

I want to tell you about healthier and happier things. I
want death later, not now.

I want

I want my wife and me to grow lettuce and kale and make mixed-green salads. I want a garden of root vegetables on the roof of our brownstone. I want a glass ceiling beneath so we can look up from a bedroom at nature and life.

I want to smell the ocean each morning. I want to hear birds at the window and gulls on a pier. I want to watch surfers glide by and magnolia petals spin in the waves like painted children doing cartwheels.

I want more music. I want more books. I want to learn to play a musical instrument neither you nor I have ever heard. I want to invent a new kind of music. I want to invent a new kind of sound. I want to invent a new kind of art.

I want to type faster. I want to write faster. I want to write by hand. I want to write a fantasy novel. I want to plug a wire into my head and have my thoughts transcribe themselves across reams and reams and reams.

I want to know if I would really want any of these things or if I just think that I do. I want to know if there's any difference.

I want television to stop so that I can stop watching it. I want the internet to stop so that I can catch up. I want to go to the movies more often. I want to go to the ballet more often. I want to go to more museums. I want to be someone who purchases works of art and then donates

them. I want to be magnificently rich and fund all the
works of artists I admire. I want to be a patron. I want my
name on all the plaques.

I want to own restaurants. I want to learn to fillet sushi. I
want to catch a catfish with my bare hands.

I want to be shipwrecked on an island and fend for myself
with coconuts and sharpened bamboo root spears.

I want to know the root of the word *canoodle*.

I want to wrestle an alligator. I want to wrestle a crocodile.
I want to compare and share the stories that come
of each match.

I want to go back to that bar on the outskirts of Baton
Rouge where a poet friend and I ate the best pork chop
sandwiches in the world. I want to know what blues was
playing on the jukebox. I want to tell you how, when the
fat man behind the bar handed us the sandwiches on saggy
paper plates, he said, Careful boys, there's bones in there.

I want season tickets for every sports team just to give
them away—I want the seats to be good, but not
embarrassingly so.

I want a coin slot in my apartment that deposits pocket
change to my checking account.

I want a bottomless pack of chewing gum. I want bottomless beer in my fridge.
I want bottomless pocketfuls of quarters.

I want to wade in a shopping mall fountain and count the wishes. I want to find the most original of the wishes and work to make it come true, because that will be the one that's most honest and truthful.

I want to wander with my family through an Eastern Washington apple orchard and, at the end of a day spent walking and hiking and resting beneath heavy branches, I want to reach the cider mill at the valley's edge and watch the sun drip goldenly out of itself.

I want to live in the middle of nowhere and shoot whiskey bottles with a six-shooter. I want to learn how to handle a gun. I want to not ever have to fire a gun.

I want to know what it's like to be shot. I want to know what it's like to be stabbed.

I want to not ever be tortured, but I want to have been tortured in the past because then I will know that I can endure any level of pain.

I want to sit on the roof of a cider mill and type on a typewriter like a retired poet. I want to type and sing what I write at the same time.

I want to type and repeat the words I Love You until the ribbon gives out. I want to keep typing the words I Am Worthy until my hands give out or the typewriter breaks.

I want to sing until my voice goes, and then comes back again.

I want to write a sentence so lovely I'll want it tattooed

across my forearm.

I want to know what it feels like to get a tattoo. I want to
know the stories behind Polynesian full-body tattoos. I
want to know the thinking of someone with tattoos
across the face.

I want to know the thinking of someone who kills another
outside of a war.

I want to know if it is possible to kill outside of war or if
any act of killing defines itself as such.

I want life after death and assurances against hell.

I want to know if there is also a death before life, just as
there may be life after death.

I want my wife to know that, with her, I am both more and
less afraid of death.

I want my wife to know that, because of her, I've never
again tried to kill myself.

I want us to be US forever, never parting.

I want you to know I mean this completely and sentimen-
tally but unabashedly and honestly and without shame.

I want to know if we love harder or if it just
seems that way.

I want to say that maybe this is just the nature of love, that
it's like granite, like glacier, for those who are really in it.

I want

I want to know how my parents really feel about me. I want to know everything about them so I can write their life stories and give a bound book to my children. I want to pass along a history of family in bottles sent out to sea.

I want to know the stories of my ancestors, of who and what and how they loved.

I want to make up these stories if I have to, but I want as much truth as possible.

I want my great-great-grandchildren to know who I was.

I want them to read this. I want them to know about the wife I loved, the places I lived, the things I did. I want them to know I had a full head of hair and that baldness does not run on my side of the family. I want them to know they should watch themselves with alcohol, because their blood was born with a craving. I want them to know they should watch themselves around knives. I want them to know how I died, if it will help them.

I want my hair to stop growing so that I never need another haircut. I want my fingernails and toenails to stop growing so I never need to trim them. I want to grow flowers. I want to know the names of all the state flowers. I want to camp in the Cascades and wake to find a herd of elk wandering through a riverbed like the reindeer my grandfather tended. I want to relive the memory I have of waking in a friend's cabin a week after Jenns died, when I went wandering to pee near the river and stumbled upon all those elk-deer drinking in the morning mist, and I wondered if maybe they had something to do with him.

I want to know if they did.

I want to watch grizzly bears paw for spawning salmon in the wild. I want to watch a bald eagle claw a red fish from a stream. I want to watch baby salmon hatching from gelly, orange eggs.

I want to spend a month in the mountains counting loons. I want to hold a male mallard in my arms, pet its green feathers, and tell it about my grandmother. I want every kind of songbird to perch for a time on my finger and sing to me. I want to have been a vegan for a year. I want to bicycle more often.

I want a bicycle of my own in the apartment. I want my wife's bicycle to be more easily accessible and weigh twenty pounds less. I want a garage. I want an attic. I want a house with a lawn and a street lined with trees. I want birds at the window and livestock in a distant pasture.

I want to ride a bull in a rodeo. I want to watch a bullfight, but I don't want anyone to get hurt. I want to organize a world tour of mutton busting. I want to know what it's like to fight a bull.

I want to go back in time to a bullfight in Spain in which both the bull and the bullfighter were killed. I want to see it happen, but I don't want it to happen again.

I want to be editor-in-chief of a prominent literary magazine. I want to live one floor higher than I do and still have a backyard. I want a new computer each time a new model's released. I want to not want technology. I want a new phone each time the next is released. I want phones and computers to stay the same. I want to not check my email. I want to not spend so much time on the computer not writing. I want the only time I spend on my computer to be the time I use writing stories for my family.

I want to take a ride in a fighter jet. I want to land a plane on an aircraft carrier. I want to run out of the tunnel at Notre Dame Stadium.

I want to spend the night in a haunted library. I want to pretend all libraries are haunted. I want all of my boyhood dreams to come true in my memory. I want a tree fort. I want an orange bike like I used to have.

I want to sit behind a wooden desk in my elementary school and listen to my teacher translate what old authors meant. I want to count the minutes on the clock above the teacher's head, the seconds ticking away with the thin red hand while subjects and predicates and verbs are explained to me.

I want to anticipate the bell's ring. I want to line up outside the door of the class. I want to walk single file through the playground and ride a school bus home. I want to count down the eight stops backwards to mine.

I want to step the first short steps down and hop the last long one to the ground. I want to walk home from the bus stop past the house with the mad German Shepherd and the new house my mother said has a nice paint job but will

never sell. I want to know if it ever sold. I want to know
how the mad shepherd died.

I want to walk more slowly past the house where the
Rohlen boys with the dirt bikes lived. I want to walk faster
past the house where the angry farmer lived. I want to
come home and do my homework at the kitchen table. I
want to drink a glass of milk and close my binder. I want
to go outside to ride my orange bike till the sun goes
down. I want to park my orange bike in the garage and
yawn and climb up the side of my red bunk bed and read
until I can't keep my eyes open. I want to dream of being
a writer living in New York City, with a beautiful woman
who loves me and a tree-lined street and a bicycle. I want
to tell that boy to keep reading.

I want to know if a truthful, believable assurance that
Everything Will Be Okay would have made me happier
as a child or if I just think it would. I want to believe that
Everything Will Be Okay because then I will sweat less. I
want you to tell me that assurances don't matter. I want
you to say, We're all going to die in the end, and there's
nothing either of us can do about it. I want you to say it so
that I can refute it, because I am doing something,
finally, right now.

I want to be reassured all the time.

I want

I want to do college over again, to relive it, but I don't want to do high school over again. I want to do elementary school again, but I don't want to do junior high again.

I want to relive the first time I hit Jenns on the football field. I want to remember if Jenns ever caught a touchdown in a game. I want to remember Jenns better than I do.

I want Gator and me to carry Jenns off the field under the lights on our shoulders. I want the crowd to go wild. I want the band to play. I want the cheerleaders to scream and high-five and kiss him.

I want to lean back against the lockers in the locker room and laugh and laugh and laugh with my teammates. I want to not care what happens next. I want to know if that's kind of like what training on Mt. Rainier was like for my grandfather, like being on a football team and not knowing a damn thing about what's next. I want to believe it might have been, if only because it would make me feel closer to my grandfather.

I want to better understand my own wantings. I want to better understand how my mind's different and the same as the minds of everyone else. I want to understand what makes my grandfather and me different people.

I want to better understand the history of philosophy. I want to be a philosopher.

I want to better understand the history of the world. I want to be a historian.

I want to better understand botany, cartography. I want to distinguish edible and inedible plant life just by where they'd be placed on a map.

I want to eat berries and leaves and the right kinds of mushrooms. I want to eat bark and pinecones and fallen fruit. I want raw meals of found flora. I want ferns and roots, nuts and bark. I want to dig wild carrots from the ground. I want to rename the flowers and weeds.

I want to understand the great nature of all breathing things in this world.

I want

I want to be an expert in everything.

I want to study katydids and ants under a magnifying glass.
I want to grow basil and herbs on a windowsill beneath a
pot rack in a beautiful kitchen you can see from the street.
I want to bring the writer and the reader closer together so
that this feels like two people with tied blood sharing
stories over coffee.

I want to bring the writer and reader closer together so
that this feels like two soldiers sharing stories over a fire.

I want to bring the writer and reader closer together so
that this feels like me and Jenns driving home from practice and taking the long way.

I want to completely change the written word, but I don't
want to do it through technological means. I want a vacation. I want to climb into a magnolia tree somewhere,
anywhere, and sleep and think about all that I already have
and how much I don't really need anything more at all.

I want to plant a magnolia tree. I want to plant acres and
acres of magnolia trees. I want to organize a guerilla art
project and cover the parking lots of closed discount shopping malls with massive potted magnolia trees in bloom. I
want to slap every bigot in America in the face. I want to
plant magnolia trees in bottles and float them down the
Hudson River, past Manhattan and out to sea. I want to
not meet hate with more hate. I want gay marriage to be

legal everywhere. I want love to be enough for anything, anywhere. I want to understand the law, but I don't want to go to law school. I want to have already gone to law school.

I want to have gone to Paris for a doctorate in French literature. I want to learn to make an enlightening pain au chocolat. I want to learn to mix cheese. I want to tell you how I learned the other day that cheddar is a verb. I want to cheddar something. I want to taste mold. I want to taste wine grapes off a Loire Valley vine. I want to learn to make wine. I want to live on a vineyard. I want to crush grapes beneath my toes. I want to feel a stem cutting between them as the sting of the sugary juices soak in.

I want to disinfect all my scrapes with heavily alcoholic wine. I want my vineyard's wines to go label-less, each bottle signed in chalk with JENNS 4 EVER by whomever's blood was spilt in its making. I want my bare feet to bleed and to mix my blood in my winemaking. I want my vineyard covered in grape stems and children's sidewalk chalk. I want a chalkboard in my workspace.

I want to write equations on an enormous chalkboard in a cavernous library. I want to listen to the scratchy echo of chalk-on-slate as it slides through the stacks.

I want to clap erasers out the windows of skyscrapers.

I want to leap from a rooftop grasping a great orange bouquet of balloons like salmon eggs, then float gently to the street.

I want to eat a hotdog bought from a street vendor. I want

to manage a halal cart for a summer lunch hour in mid-town. I want to sell ice cream in Central Park. I want to sell acrylic board paintings of flowers sculpted from orange snow in front of a museum. I want to sell used notebooks from bottles along the Seine.

I want to paddle a gondola in Venice. I want to blow glass in Murano. I want to build a chandelier to pass down through my family. I want a grandfather clock with pink-stained glass for its face, and I want it to refract the clock hands in such a way that time is always wrong in a lovelier way than right.

I want to spend an evening drinking scotch with a watchmaker.

I want to make locks and keys more interesting. I want to make locks and keys ornately, skeletal. I want to not ever need lock a thing. I want to unlock all the secrets I keep from myself. I want to get my life organized. I want a cleaner house and a cleaner mind. I want to always be able to find what I'm looking for. I want to always know what it is I'm looking for.

I want to uncover a treasure map to a time capsule I hid as a boy. I want to find the alphabet blocks I used to write simple sentences with as a toddler. I want to know what I wrote with those blocks. I want to inhale the smell of a fresh box of ninety-six crayons. I want to finger-paint the walls of my apartment. I want to color in all the white space. I want to draw family portraits in cerulean and red-orange and pink.

I want to draw monsters and space aliens. I want to use the

cerulean down to its nub coloring an ocean. I want a burnt
sienna island and a midnight blue sky. I want the whole
room to smell of waxy crayon. I want to add magnolia
trees blooming from the water and two surfers paddling
through them. I want to draw a desert island with a single
pine tree in place of palm. I want to decorate the desert
island pine with Christmas lights and presents. I want to
add reindeer and a boy standing with them while orange
snow falls on the ocean all around.

I want to open a deli where meat is wrapped in holiday
wrapping paper. I want glow-in-the-dark wrapping paper
for my children at Christmas. I want the kids to sneak out
their rooms the night before and see the gifts glowing
there fresh from Santa's workshop, northern
lights emanating off.

I want a model globe full of dirt. I want a blank model
globe I can color in with crayon. I want to make the world
a more beautiful place to live.

I want you to buy me a beer. I want to play softball for
a company team. I want to play darts in a Dublin pub. I
want to go to the Olympics. I want to carry the torch.

I want to eat a sandwich on the Spanish steps in Rome.
I want to attend mass at St. Peter's. I want to believe in
Jesus. I want to believe in Moroni. I want to believe in
Mohammed. I want to believe in Buddha. I want to ac-
cept the blessings of the Dalai Lama. I want to reach the
highest level of Scientology and learn all its secrets. I want
to believe in all the Hindu and Roman and ancient gods. I
want to call on them by name. I want to make sacrifices.

I want to believe in something so strongly I'd drink from any cup set before me.

I want to feel absolute protection. I want to feel an absolute holiness. I want to feel an absolute spirituality. I want to feel absolution. I want to levitate with faith. I want to know if absolute belief in religion is different than absolute belief in love. I want you to know the feeling of absolute love.

I want to not believe in global warming. I want the world to be a safer place. I want to walk in Antarctica and leave permanent prints in the snow.

I want to dance on the North Pole. I want to watch a ballerina go *on pointe* at the top of Mount Everest. I want to watch a polar bear swim to safety with its cub on its back and an orca breaching behind.

I want an orca to leap over me as I stand on a spiral jetty.

I want to spend a day watching the grass grow. I want to relive a rainy November high school football practice. I want to relive breaking my leg playing defense senior year. I want to replay every high school football game except one. I want to replay three high school basketball games.

I want to know what happened to my car after I sold it.

I want a vanity license plate so clever every other driver wishes they'd thought of it first.

I want to know if the person who bought my car treated it well. I want to tell them about the people who've ridden in it.

I want to tell them about Jenns.

I want to tell them about Gator.

I want to tell them about me.

I want

I want to tell you about Ginger, my pup, a beagle-terrier mix, twenty-something pounds. I want to tell you about my sister's dog, a bit bigger, Juno, an uncertain browner breed than Ginger. I want to tell you how Ginger had red bubbles at the corners of her eyes, how the terrier side of her made her snout snort and snot. I want to tell you how Juno had front paws that turned outwards like mallard feet, whiskers like a cat and brown eyes like a person's. I want to tell you about the time I walked into the dining room and found Juno standing on top of the table eating a stick of butter, while Ginger cowered below, trying to hide between the legs of a chair.

I want to tell you how Ginger slept in my bed even after I left for college and how she'd dream sometimes she was chasing something or digging somewhere. I want to know what she was digging for, or to.

I want to tell you how Ginger and Juno used to compete for space in front of the gas fireplace and would always end up in a pile, panting.

I want to tell you how Ginger was underfed wherever she was born, and for the whole of her life she ate whatever food was placed before her as fast as she could, growling if anyone got near. I want to tell you how if you walked past Ginger while she was eating, she'd lash out like a snake striking, then retreat and eat faster, barely able to breath. I want to tell you how she did this to my grandfather once and he laughed and said it reminded him of children he saw in the war.

I want to tell you how a person could walk right up to
Juno while she was eating and just take her food.

I want to tell you how both dogs knew words, like *Food*
and *Walk* and *Treat* and *Juno* and *Ginger* and *Home*.

I want to tell you how Ginger knew the word *Joe*
but Juno didn't.

I want to tell you how Ginger could dance on her hind legs
but would never jump. I want to tell you how Juno could
jump higher than the length of her body
but couldn't dance.

I want to tell you how Juno died first, of cancer, aged
almost 91 in dog years, and how then Ginger died three
days later, even though she was much younger and hadn't
been sick at all.

I want to tell you about the veterinarian, who cremated the
Valley's dead pets and spread their ashes on Mt. Rainier.
I want to visit the spot where Ginger's ashes were spread
and lay a wreath of pig ears and chew toys.

I want to visit the spot where Juno's ashes were spread and
lay a warm blanket and stick of butter.

I want to know how far these spots are from where my
grandfather camped.

I want to know how far these graves are from Santa Claus'
summer home.

I want

I want to see my grandmother at least one more time
before she dies. I want to share coffee with her and record
our conversation. I want to know how she remembers her
life and what moments she would relive if she could.

I want to know if my grandfather wrote letters to her
while away at war. I want to know if he kept a notebook.
I want to know if he wrote poems or songs, if he sang
Christmas carols with the other soldiers during a break in
the fighting, if he sent bottles with notes inside
them out to sea.

I want to tell you how, after nearly four years of training,
my grandfather's division landed in Italy on Christmas Eve
to join the bloodier part of the war.

I want to know if Christmas in Italy, 1944, was a
white Christmas.

I want to know how many stars shining then are
still shining now.

I want to know if my grandmother ever had a sense of
dread, late at night, that her husband was in danger, and I
want to know if at that same moment, all the way across
the world, he was caught in the midst of a firefight.

I want to know how many men my grandfather killed. I
want to know the details of every mission he fought. I
want to hold the packs and rations he carried through Italy

in 1944. I want to fire his gun. I want to wear his helmet.
I want to know if he kept anything with him for luck, like
bible verses or a picture of my grandmother.

I want to share a breakfast with my grandfather and his
platoon during the war, when he was younger than I am
now and already doing more than I've done. I want to
drink coffee with them and laugh with them. I want to
know what they would relive if they could.

I want to hear their stories of the worst of it, the bonding
and brotherhood the only good, and the shaving of heads
and dying of friends.

I want to know a friendship rooted in risking lives. I want
to tell them about football and Jenns, about the best friend
who stuck his fingers down my throat to save me.

I want to cross-country ski through a Woods at nighttime.
I want to chart a course by compass, navigation by
gut and luck and stars.

I want to narrowly escape an explosion. I want to hear
the sounds of falling bombs. I want to drop for cover and
pray, to dig inside my helmet for a rosary or talisman, to
hear over the cataclysm the prayers of all my brothers
who surround me.

I want to tie tourniquets and grasp bloody hands. I want to
learn the Last Rites by heart.

I want to watch a house façade open up and explode like
the disembowelling of a dollhouse.

I want to rebuild a house with my bare hands. I want to
sail a boat with thick ropes and instinct. I want to hammer
a nail into a fencepost with my fist. I want to tap a maple
tree for syrup and make breakfasts for troops in
ugly, bloody snow.

I want to write letters to the past. I want to pen-pal with
troops all over the war, in Africa and Italy and London
under bombs. I want accounts of the pyramids and swimming in the Nile. I want descriptions of the Duomo and
wines from damp cellars. I want songbooks of the carols
sung at Westminster Abbey during Christmas 1944.

I want to know the hopes and dreams a man might find
when his life is in constant danger as he travels
through a distant land.

I want to send thank you cards and birthday cards and
get-well-soon cards. I want to send Christmas cards and
postcards. I want to be better at keeping in touch with
people, and I want to feel it's worth the effort.

I want to not feel that friendships are transient. I want to
not feel that friendships are replaceable.

I want to not take these bonds for granted anymore.

I want a new Ginger and Juno for my children to love.

I want to know what Ginger and Juno thought of us.

I want

I want to travel to Scotland in the rain with my wife and our family. I want to visit Iceland in the summer when the sun never sets and again in the winter when the sun never rises. I want to experience a daylong night so we have time to count all the stars.

I want to experience a nighttime day. I want us to dream and walk backwards in time along the pink-purple ribbons of never-before-seen northern lights.

I want to lay a blanket on a sand dune for a picnic with my wife and watch the pyramids being built. I want to take a late afternoon swim in a Nile lined with magnolia trees in full blossom.

I want us to share a bottle of wine outside the Santa Maria Novella and watch the setting of the capstone on the Duomo.

I want us to light evening candles at medieval vespers in Westminster abbey.

I want us to write more love letters. I want us to hold hands on a bridge until morning.

I want you to tell me it's okay to write something as solipsistic as this. I want you to tell me it's okay to write something as narcissistic and selfish as this.

I want to live near a bar where my best friends gather once

a week to play pool and shoot darts and laugh.

I want to brew my own beer. I want to have long breakfasts.

I want you to tell me these things, however minor, have
value and matter.

I want my writing to have value. I want it to matter.

I want you to keep reading to the end. I want you to enjoy
what you're reading. I want you to identify with this.

I want to know if you've ever had a dog.

I want to know—did it know the word *Home?*

I want

I want to know how many people have died in the time it took me to write this book.

I want to know how many will die in the time it takes you to read it.

I want to know what that comparison means about writing versus reading. I want to know if it's true one is more deadly than the other.

I want

I want you to get something out of this.

I want you to have enjoyed reading this. I want you to become my fan in spite of my solipsism.

I want you to become my fan even if you hate the look of a magnolia tree in bloom, even if you hate grandparents and families and football and dogs.

I want to edit out the self-reflexive portions of this.

I want

I want to remember my childhood speech therapy better.

I want to know what my voice sounded like before
it got fixed.

I want to relive my childhood bullydom. I want to know
why *bullydom* makes more sense as a word than *bullyhood*. I
want to know why *childdom* seems so strange as a word. I
want to know the difference between *freehood* and *freedom*.

I want people to stop using the term *navel-gazing*. I want
people to stop using the word *pontificate*. I want people to
stop using the word *innovative*.

Part Three

I want

I want to know the fear of being a soldier. I want to know the honor of being a soldier.

I want to feel I have a country worth fighting for. I want to know for whom I would die beyond my wife. I want to know if I would die for a cause.

I want to know what horrors of war would compel me to join the military. I want to know how long I would last at Normandy or Dresden.

I want to know the sound of a baby grand piano having been dropped from a building.

I want to know the sound of a piano exploded by a bomb.

I want to know the sounds of babies crying under bombings.

I want to know how it would be to live with Nazi ancestors.

I want the sins of past generations to be forgiven in those who've descended.

I want to know if I could last as a war journalist. I want to know if I could last as anything.

I want to tell you how, when I met my wife, we were working at the same newspaper. I want to tell you how she was

the editor and I was a columnist in trouble for fictionaliz-
ing an article about a love song.

I want to tell you how we argued over the spelling of the
name Elizabeth in the song's title. I want to tell you how
she was right and I was wrong.

I want to know how many soldiers died with unsent
letters in their pockets.

I want

I want to know if I would have fallen in love with a nurse during the war. I want to know what victory in Europe felt like for those who lived through enough.

I want to dig a foxhole. I want to have avoided trench foot.

I want to know the taste of army rations after a twenty-mile march and the relief of a warm stew in winter.

I want to have been an army surgeon. I want to steer a battleship or submarine. I want to ride shotgun in a flying fortress.

I want to liberate a death camp. I want to write letters home to my wife. I want to come home with a duffel over my shoulder and a loose-fitting uniform hanging off my new, more skeletal self.

I want

I want to take a bullet for someone better than myself.

I want to watch a terrified private reach a cigarette, orange-lit and tremory, above a trench to tempt snipers.

I want to call that act courageous.

I want to know what I would have done, hugging my gun in the mud.

I want to know if I would have missed on the first shot.

I want to march for something good.

I want

I want to tell you about the exchange student girl who
only went to our high school for a year. I want to tell you
how I only remember her still because of the time she did
cartwheels down the hallway, not caring if
anyone got in her way.

I want to tell you how people made fun of her and said it
was stupid but how I thought it was the coolest thing.

I want to know why she did it and if she ever did it again,
wherever she came from, whatever home she went back to.

I want

I want to make art of doing good deeds. I want to make
art of healing wounds. I want to tell the wartime injured—
you're going home.

I want to sit invisibly on 1940's front porches and watch
the faces of loved ones arriving home early and alive.

I want to feed the hungry. I want to cure the sick. I want to
make you more comfortable in whatever position you're
in while reading this.

I want to plant a magnolia tree outside the window nearest
you so you have something beautiful to look at when you
stretch your back.

I want

I want to get stronger.

I want to know torture and genocide and holocaust and burning-at-the-stake and disembowelment. I want to know drowning and water-boarding and electrocution and electroshock therapy. I want to know how it feels to resist these things, to live through these things, to perform these things, to have loved ones who've endured these things.

I want forgiveness for my family's past wrongs and still-coming wrongs. I want to relive my wrongs. I want to relive the grand totality of human experience. I want to breathe as you breathe, and I want our hearts to beat to-gether as we sing old love songs together as loud as we can.

I want to know what will make you cry. I want you to feel the tears building behind your eyes.

I want you to feel your grandfather's hand on your shoulder.

I want you to feel love swelling in your heart.

I want you to feel a favorite blanket wrapped around you and inhale deeply, deeply, deeply through your nose.

I want

I want to be saved.

I want to be born again, again. I want to relive the years
I was a believer.

I want to tell you how, after Jenns died, some of us brothers from the football team went looking for answers in a
Christian youth group. I want to tell you how we didn't
find what we were looking for, but we found fellowship,
and guitars, and a better goodness than we knew existed.

I want to tell you how, my hands clasped in prayer and
eyes closed in a church basement, I raised my hand and
said Yes. I want to tell you how I wanted, at that moment,
nothing more than to commit to my life to the love of
Jesus, or whatever this goodness was I'd discovered amidst
these football players and friends. I want to tell you how
good it felt, to just give away all that hurting and be
accepted, be protected.

I want to reread the Bible, but only the monologues, the
bits about peace and the beauty of the weak. I want to
reread the Psalms, the wonderful poetry of it. I want to
reread the Gospel of Luke, the less-impressed impression
he had of Jesus, which seems somehow more honest than
the more praising books.

I want to tell you how I still believe, I think, somewhere
deep down, but I want to tell you that what I believe in
now is Love, with an initial capitalization, Love like God.

Love like the sound of open-E guitar with
brand new strings.

I want to tell you how, the first time our ex-football-coach-
turned-preacher said, God is Love, it was the first time I
actually heard it. I want to tell you how I'd heard it said in
Sunday school so many times, but it took Jenns' second
shot for it to hit me.

I want to spend a summer afternoon painting posts in
a raspberry field and singing praise songs alone.

I want to spend a summer morning picking blueberries. I
want to make you a pie to eat while you read this. I want
you to spill the juices on the pages and make this text colorful as blood or coral or salmon roe.

I want to live on a beach of orange sand. I want to run in
the ocean with my pup Ginger alive again. I want to spend
a day as a seagull gliding on warm wind currents. I want
to learn the nomenclature of cloud types. I want to know
the names of all the constellations and teach them to my
kids. I want to invent constellations. I want to draw my
children's names and faces in heavens that will never burn
out and show them their portraits painted in space. I want
to draw my grandparents' names in different stars and ask
my children to please remember. I want to paint our family
constellations on the ceilings of bedrooms. I want guests
to ask me to show them the faces in the stars and I want to
say, There, there, and there.

I want

I want to lie on the beach and map out a voyage by celestial navigation. I want epic adventures I can make into great stories for my children at bedtime.

I want to know a little bit about everything. I want to ride an elephant through the jungle. I want to use a banana leaf as an umbrella and a tidal pool as a bath. I want to shower in a waterfall and dry on the moss. I want to live amongst the gorillas and speak to them in sign. I want to watch a chimpanzee translate my stories. I want to write with the voice of a lion. I want to pet a live tiger. I want to ride an elk like a cowboy. I want to ski behind horses like my forebears did. I want to know the truth behind the sasquatch. I want to run with my grandfather's reindeer through the tundra. I want to captain a dogsled. I want to spend a night in an igloo.

I want to ride along on a government-sanctioned traditional whaling expedition. I want to go back in time and see how they whaled then.

I want to paddle a cedar canoe out to sea with my bare hands. I want to watch the scapula twitch of the harpooner. I want to watch the arc and yaw of the throw. I want to feel the thrill of the strike, the lurch and the roar. I want to see magnolia petals in the whitewater spray. I want to taste humpback.

I want to tell you how I spent my summers during college on an island in the San Juans, near Canada, and how early

one evening I went out rowing and saw so many orcas near
Battleship Island, spouting round the kayak I floated in,
mid-pod, no motor.

I want to tell you how a bald eagle looked down on the
whales from a tree and how maybe it saw nothing but all
those salmon the whales were chasing, but how maybe it
was wishing it were not a bird but a whale instead, capable
to eat as many salmon as it wished in a single,
more powerful bite.

I want to tell you how I was wishing I were an eagle right
then instead of a boy with an oar and how the voices of
the whales were so many and whiny and tinny and audible
from my floating place above them that I could hear them
calling out about me. I want to tell you how I had no idea
what the whales were thinking but that it was probably not
that they were wishing to be me or an eagle or anything
other than a grand and beautiful whale.

I want

I want to know about the native wars before the white man
landed in America. I want to know if theirs was a more
peaceful nature or a more warful one. I want to know how
often children died. I want to know the creation stories
and anecdotes, their non-scientific explanation for snow
and for stars. I want to know
about their god or Gods.

I want to tell you how, still in the closet at my parents'
house, is the blanket the nurses wrapped me in at the hospital when I was born. I want to tell you how whenever I
go home at the holidays I take it out for a moment and run
the silky fringe between my fingers and feel like crying.

I want

I want to go back to being eight years old and riding in my grandfather's work van. I want to relive butterscotch hard candies and singing Finnish folks songs phonetically. I want to share a flat of wild cherries and spit the pits at parked cars.

I want to relive our ride to that fishing spot, the sun rising pink-purple over the evergreens, and I want to tell you how some mornings at my grandparents' lake house the air could be so cold and wet that the trees' needles turned blue. I want to tell you how we would wake into that early morning mist and fog and go out into the trees on a digging trip for earthworms.

I want to tell you how we would empty a gallon-sized coffee can of bent nails and rusted screws onto a cold garage floor at dawn. I want to tell you how we would fill the coffee can with wet dirt and worms, how it was my job to carry the worms down to the dock while my grandfather left a note in the kitchen and pocketed us cookies for breakfast. I want to tell you how the cookies always tasted of fish and dirt and butterscotch.

I want to remember the words of those Finnish songs my grandfather sang while we ate cookies in the rowboat. I want to know what kind of song it was so that I might in some way rewrite it for guitar.

I want to know if the song my grandfather sang was a war song or a love song, fight song or pop song, holiday

or drinking, camp song or soul song, swing song or heart
song or sing-a-long psalm song. I want to know where he
learned it. I want to know who sang it first.

I want a recording of my grandfather singing his song. I
want to know that you can give something life if
you want it enough.

I want

I want to meet my ancestors and find in them what has passed down to my sister and me. I want to find what was lost in translation.

I want memories of the places in my life that I wasn't. I want to tell you how, when my grandfather's sister visited from Finland, they were both in their eighties. I want to tell you how I only remember her a little, having coffee with the rest of the adults around the kitchen table at the lake house while my grandfather translated in a shaky voice, his Parkinson's present already.

I want to tell you how, what I remember most of my grandfather's sister, was the story of she and my grandfather saying goodbye at the Seattle airport. I want to tell you how they were both so old and my grandfather was so sick already that just a drive to the airport was exhausting. I want to tell you how they knew this airport goodbye was goodbye for good.

I want to know what it's like to say goodbye to somebody like that.

I want to tell you how, even though I wasn't there for it, I remember this goodbye very clearly. I want to know what they said to each other. I want to know if she sang the same song my grandfather sang to her grandchildren. I want to know if there were spiders hiding in the walls.

I want to know what I would say to my sister.

I want

I want a memory of the snowy morning my sister was born, when I was not yet two years old. I want to tell you how, in pictures, I'm shown scarfing Christmas cookies greedily with pink-scrubbed nurses at their station. I want to tell you how my sister was born on Christmas morning and how my mother says it was snowing outside the windows of the maternity ward but not on the ground twenty-some floors below. I want to tell you how she said it was special snow just for us, and how I replied, I wish the special snow was orange.

I want a memory of the doctor who delivered me. I want to meet the nurse who swaddled me. I want to meet the emergency room resident who stitched up my legs and elbows after I crashed my orange bike on the neighbor's driveway.

I want to spend an afternoon shooting my old BB gun at pop cans off the fence in my parents' backyard. I want to know why I now say *soda* in conversation but still write *pop* when I think of it. I want to finally do a keg stand. I want to climb a jungle gym. I want a swing set.

I want

I want to play worship songs on the Isaac Stern stage at Carnegie Hall.

I want you to sit in the back row of the balcony while I stand in the middle of the stage—let's see how quiet we can whisper and still hear each other.

I want

I want to hang high above the city and watch how it works people like blood cells and avenues like arteries—Central Park like a belly and Spuyten Duyvil like a brain.

I want

I want to share everything beautiful I ever experience.

I want to share everything horrible I ever experience.

I want to compound the world together into
one massive verb.

I want to tell you about the time my sister and I tore a
sliver of wallpaper off the lake house guest bathroom by
accident, and I don't remember how we tore off the piece,
but I do remember that we colored the floral print back
together with crayons. I want to tell you how that was the
first moment I remember my sister and me working together as a team. I want to tell you how we got away with it
completely and how the part we colored in is still there at
the lake house because no one ever uses
that bathroom anyway.

I want to tell you how, even though she lives across the
country now, I feel closer to my sister now than I
did when we were kids.

I want to tell you how the lake house is for sale now.

I want

I want to tell you how my grandfather used to say that the only real coffee in this world is brewed from Finnish dirt, That is the only real black coffee, he'd say, ground of ground, born from earth.

I want to roast my own coffee from the dirt below the subways, the muck of New York City's underground. I want to go to Seattle and do the same.

I want to go to Ireland and drink tea brewed of clover-leaves with my wife. I want to drink in the Puyallup River as it flows off Mount Rainier. I want to breathe in the smell of exhaled history. I want to start my day grounded deep in my past and then make something real with my hands.

I want to live life like a farmer. I want to slaughter my own pork belly and bacon. I want to milk my own cow. I want to master macramé. I want to know if macramé and matrimony are related, if that phrase, Tying the knot, was born of a shared root.

I want life and life and more life. I want to plant seeds and watch them grow. I want blood gone green and pink-purple with a great beating heart full of love. I want to see the hearts beating in everything.

I want to see hearts in the faces of strangers. I want to step onto a subway car and hear the thump-thumping of all beating life. I want to walk every subway tunnel and

read all the graffiti. I want to read all the poems no one has
seen since their writing. I want to read all the letters that
dissolved in the surf at Normandy. I want to sing paragraphs aloud in Finnish while fishing.

I want to paint graffiti on the belly of an airplane. I want it
to say, *This is navelgazing.*

I want to tell you about the afternoon in 1989 when my
sister wrote 'i HaT MoM' across the walls of our house
in permanent marker. I want to tell you how my mother
didn't say a word when she saw it but just went to her
bedroom and shut the door. I want to tell you how when
I got hungry I didn't know what to do. I want to tell you
how my mother didn't come out, even when I knocked and
asked her about dinner. I want to tell you how scary it was,
being six years old with a mom in her room with the door
shut and the sun still shining.

I want to tell you how my sister was just barely five and
hiding in her room too. I want to tell you how I was surprised she could spell as well as she did. I want to tell you
how that was the first time I ever cooked dinner for myself, some kind of canned pasta and toast, and I even did
my own dishes and washed my own pot. I want to tell you
how when my father got home I was smiling and happy
and proudly doing homework at the kitchen table. I want
to tell you how I was showing him what a grown up boy I
could be, how I could do all this living and person-being
on my own, without anyone telling me how, but all he saw
was what my sister had written, or what maybe he thought
I had written, so I want to tell you how I was confused
when he came up the stairs faster than ever, wanting to
know what had happened, but I didn't remember what he

was talking about, had forgotten the writing my sister had
made because I was so proud of the dinner I'd cooked,
and so I just said, I know how to make dinner now,
do you want some?

I want to tell you how, for Mother's Day in 1990, my sister
painted 'I love MoM' on the wall of the garage and how I
helped her do it so it would be spelt right.

I want

I want experience, more than anything, and to feel that I've not wasted my chances at being a person who mattered.

I want to write something great on the belly of a plane and send it out soaring over the world.

I want to run alongside the Wright brothers in that North Carolina field.

I want to work alongside Gutenberg and watch him print his Bibles. I want to start my own publishing press and handprint every copy.

I want to gaze up at the belly of a graphitized plane as it flies fast and low over me.

I want to live through an unpredictable airline explosion.

I want to touch raw chicken with my bare hands.

I want to watch a bald eagle steal a salmon from the mouth of an orca.

I want to leap from a brownstone into a pile of orange leaves. I want to carry orange leaves and pink petals in black bags and release them from city rooftops. I want to watch them float down and get carried away like a flock of pink swallows flying warm in orange snow.

I want all the city's trees to grow taller than its buildings. I

want limbs over rooftops and petals on the streets. I want
water-tower blossoms and Empire State stems. I want
sunlight through a canopy and no traffic at all.

I want you to know that what you want from life doesn't
have to make sense, and maybe it's best if it doesn't.

I want

I want to know how great we can be if we let ourselves. I want to know how many cartwheels I could do in sequence. I want to know how much I can love, how much wanting and heart I have in me.

I want to know if that's why I started writing this book.

I want to know if that's the sentence I've been writing toward.

I want

I want to know if you're still reading, if it even matters how I end this.

I want to say what I haven't said yet.

I want to know who you are. I want to know to whom I've been writing this whole time.

I want to know how deep I could have tunneled with a shovel in my childhood backyard if my parents hadn't stopped me.

I want to know if I could have reached China.

I want to know whatever happened to those earthworm coffee cans and pocket knives, my orange bike, Jenns' parents, Gator's razor, the Ruehlin boys' dirt bikes.

I want to know if that's really a magnolia tree in front of the brownstone on 22nd Street or some other kind of tree and I got confused.

I want to know how much Finnish dirt it takes to brew a real cup of coffee.

I want to know what kind of spiders they were.

I want to know if that nail's still there.

I want to apologize for anything you didn't like, but I

wouldn't really mean it.

I want to, but I can't.

I want

I want to walk along the jogging path of the Central Park reservoir holding hands with my wife.

I want it to be the middle of the night. I want it to be cold like it's about to snow. I want us to watch the small lake turn salty and sparkly with beautiful tropical fish.

Because I want us to listen for reindeer and pack-mules hoofing in from the Great Lawn.

Because I want us to watch orcas and salmon spout from a great coral fountain at the center of the reservoir as if from a giant heart. Because I want the whales and fish to be pink and white as magnolias blown from glass.

Because I want us to walk through orange snow with the reindeer and mules. Because I want us to sing out praise songs and see our future child cartwheeling ahead.

Because I want, if nothing else, for you to understand how much we love.

Because that's why.

April 2012 – September 2013
New York City; Berlin; Seattle; Los Angeles

Because
I want to thank you.

I want to thank Polly Bresnick for being the greatest poet-agent. I want to thank Kevin Sampsell, Chloe Caldwell, Amber Sparks, Gabriel Blackwell, Jamie Iredell, and Roy Kesey for their early blessings and support. I want to thank Kyle Muntz and Michael Seidlinger for their editorial guidance and stewardship. I want to thank Daniel Long for telling it to me straight. I want to thank Penina Roth for the party. I want to thank Sean Doyle for the letter.

I want to thank *you*.

CPSIA information can be obtained at www.ICGtesting.com
Printed in the USA
BVOW01s1124070314

346973BV00002B/12/P